THE
OTHER
WORLD

BY AMARA BEA GLAVIN

PART 1: JULY 18TH, 10:38AM

There have been way too many times where I was pissed off for the most irrational reasons. Once, I almost punched someone in the grocery store for looking at me too long. I mean, I was only twelve so it's not like I would have gotten in deep trouble, and it wouldn't be that impressive. The only reason I didn't was because after I passed them, and I turned around, they were already too far away. To be fair though, it was a tall, painfully awkward looking man that had no business looking at a twelve-year-old. Period.

During my sister Veena's funeral, I wasn't mad at the old Pastor or Minister man (I didn't know the difference, and I didn't care.) who was talking about her as if he ever met her. I wasn't mad at her asshole boss who randomly showed up as if he cared. I wasn't mad at the world. I wasn't even currently mad at whoever was responsible for her death. I kid you not, I was mad at the goddamn sun. Why, oh why was it *shining*? Usually, for this type of situation,

I would say to myself, "Because it hates you, Nova. *Everything and everybody hates you!*"

Not only am I not a fan of light in general, but the fact that there was brightness coming from any direction on such a gut-wrenching, gloomy day, made me angrier than the day my grandfather told me that my paintings were never going to be past amateur level and art was only for people who didn't believe in the "American Dream", whatever that was. To be fair, he was right. I gave up on that dream when I was maybe eight.

Besides my irrational anger, that day wasn't filled with the worst emotion of my life. Why would it? That would be the day that my sister was actually killed in her car accident. The day that my dad and my mom both had to receive different phone calls saying my sister died in an ambulance after being the victim of a hit and run. That was Friday, and this was the next Thursday.

The day before the funeral, at least three of my classmates asked me if it "hit me" yet. (I say at least three because a girl from school sent an Instagram message to me apologizing with three extremely unnecessarily long paragraphs that probably included something about it "hitting me" yet, but I wasn't sure and I didn't really care.) But I kept responding with, "Yeah, no. My older sister just dramatically perished with no one there to save her, before I fell to the floor, bled my eyes to no end, and didn't open my mouth to eat anything, or talk for the next three days. But NOOOOO. Totally hasn't 'hit me' yet."

No shit it had "hit me". What people really should have been asking was if it had *resonated* with me yet. That would have made a lot more sense, because obviously no. We hadn't had any holidays without her yet. We hadn't celebrated either of our graduations without her yet. I hadn't come home to tell her good news without her there to hear it yet. I hadn't tried to call her while knowing she wasn't gonna pick up yet. So, no. No resonation for me just yet.

That was gonna take a while, which honestly helped me during her funeral. I was okay with not having closure after a two-hour service. My parents on the other hand, they were both adamant on having it straight away.

My parents divorced when I was five, and honestly there were never really any issues, until my sister's funeral that is.

"Nova!" My mom called out to me, beckoning me towards her. "You're gonna ride with me in the limo."

"Why isn't Dad coming?" I asked. Considering she was, you know, his daughter too. If he wanted to ride in the limo with her casket, damn it he was gonna.

"He, um, said he didn't want to. And besides, Ralph is riding with us. It'll be way too squished."

Bullshit.

"Are you really being that egotistical right now? At Veena's funeral?"

"Hey," my dad yelled out, walking up to us. "Are we ready to go?"

"Mom said you're riding somewhere else."

Dad wiped his hands over his face like he always did before he tried and failed to not raise his voice. Dad tried, don't get me wrong. He just absolutely sucked at it.

"Charlotte, I thought we discussed we're all going in the limo?"

Ralph gave me the look that said, "Don't get involved, just let it go. It'll be fine." Ralph was an amazing stepdad. He always had my back, and supported everything I did. When Veena died the week before, it was him that I went up to crying first, but at that very moment, I ignored everything he was trying to tell me through his dramatic facial language.

"We are all going in the limo end of discussion," I assertively announced as I shoved myself into the backseat. Why was this even a conversation? My parents never even truly fought, but they chose *now* to not get along? Both of them have always been stubborn, but I thought they would have at least some compassion for each other at their daughter's funeral.

Funeral. Geez, what a pathetic word for something so dark. It never felt appropriate to me. Like the word "fart" is totally appropriate for its meaning, or the word "vomit". That all fits, but "funeral" sounds too elegant, and not messy enough. I didn't want to feel elegant after Veena had been hit by some idiot driving in the wrong lane. Even when we cover up the messy parts of a hit and run, nothing will ever make me stop replaying what that must have been like for her over and over again.

Anyway, after I threw myself into the overly fancy, black vehicle, I figured everyone would follow me into it. We were holding everyone up and it was time to leave. But no. Obviously. The three of them continued to talk about whatever for at least two long minutes before joining me. Behavior like this wasn't rare. At all. Keep in mind, I was fifteen, not eight. Some people consider listening to their child when they have almost relevant things to say, but that attitude toward your children is like posting a picture on Instagram; You're probably just doing it to make yourself feel better.

I'm constantly ignored by people in general. I'm expected to go to school for eight hours a day, do more homework for two more hours, play sports, participate in an art, be social, eat healthy, clean pretty much the entire house in both of my households, all at the age of fifteen. But have an opinion on a simple gesture and empathetic behavior? How dare I.

Before I knew it, we were on the road from the funeral home to the church. I hated churches. I had nothing against freedom of religion or whatever crap American religious people constantly say when trying to force their religion on me, but that wasn't my issue. Churches just always had a talent for making me feel uncomfortable. First, I hate crowds. Many people wouldn't guess that by looking at my black clothing and purple hair. Some family members are still convinced I am destined to grow up in a rock band, spending my days and nights in a trashy club while smoking meth or however you ingest the substance that could be a liquid for all I know. Second, I hate touching people, and people touching me. Don't you dare put a piece of nasty ass candy directly from your filthy fingers into my mouth. And yes, you heard me right. CANDY. Whatever those people call it; bread, body of Christ. That's fine and all, but it's freaking candy. And third, I didn't easily get along with many other kids my age. I don't know why, it was just always hard for me.

During the few times that I went to church as a kid with my grandparents, I always glued myself to the back of Veena. If she cared in the slightest, she never told me. She seemed fairly content with having me around, but her friends sure seemed to care. I was usually referred to as "Veena's obnoxious little sister." And the most pathetic part was, most of them really did try and be nice to me...sometimes. Veena's closest friend, Raya, NEVER had a single nice thing to say about me, but she's not worth talking about. But hot damn, was it hard. I was a brat, and I will fully admit it, and that is my whole point. The only person's company I really enjoyed as a kid was Veena's. Thank God she eventually introduced me to my only real friend, Jack. Veena was one of the few people in our small school that instantly knew Jack was gay. This was useful for two reasons; he wouldn't try to be a prick to me, and he felt like an outsider too. She figured we would understand each other, and she was absolutely right.

Jack was the first person to greet me at the church when I stepped outside of the limo. I asked him to do that. As much as I love my grandparents, I would never be prepared to see their faces as they watched me get out of a limo with my deceased sister in the back. This wasn't supposed to be how they finished the last years of their lives.

From the time I walked up the stairs, to the time we scattered dirt and roses onto my sister's casket, I had trouble hearing. It sounds strange, but it was more like I wasn't listening to what people were saying to me, or what songs people were singing. Maybe I just couldn't activate my hearing sense, or whatever. Or maybe it was just that goddamn sun. Bitch.

My parents finally stopped being pricks and all came together after the ceremony ended and people were just sobbing, in silence. My dad, John, and Ralph always had an appreciation for each other. I guess they just had similar experiences in life, especially now. They wrapped their arms around each other while I squeezed Jack's hand. Damn, Jack knew me well. He knew not to say a single thing during the ceremony. What on Earth was I supposed to say in return? There wasn't anything to say. I knew he was sorry, and that he was always there for me. That's why I wouldn't have been able to get through this without him. Everyone else was sure as hell saying that crap to me. Not that I wasn't appreciative of their compassion, it was just annoying.

I began to feel more conscious during the reception where people felt like they could be at least a little bit more joyful. Everyone exchanged their favorite stories of Veena in private conversations with each other. Laughter felt like it was being squeezed out of everyone with a tear or two following each crack of a smile.

From what I saw during the reception, most people were afraid to come up and talk to me. Made sense. Most of my family knew I didn't deal with emotions well, and what does one say to the younger sister of their most likely favorite family member? "Sorry about your sister, I feel bad that we got along with her a lot better than you"? I didn't care, and not that I was shocked in any way, but I was just happy that my sister made such an impact in people's lives. The reception at a funeral should always be a reflection on how the deceased made us feel. So it was appropriate that people were social, joyous, and supportive of one another.

As I glued my butt to the couch for most of the afternoon, Jack kept voluntarily waiting on me hand and foot by repeatedly bringing me root beer floats. I swear I'm gonna lose all my teeth one day specifically because of this crap, but it's *my* crap. My *favorite* crap. It was probably my mom's idea to serve it, she'd been babying me even before my sister passed. And who serves ice cream at a funeral?

"Wanna listen to music?" Jack asked me as he brought over my third root beer float.

"No, it's okay," I responded, still looking forward. The numbness in my ears apparently traveled to my eyes. It was getting hard to control them, even if I only wanted to blink. "I just think my mom would yell at me if I had headphones in."

"Yeah, you're right. Stupid me." Jack pushed his glasses back and snapped his focus to his lap. I wasn't sure why he thought I would get mad at him. He should have known he's usually the only person I didn't regularly think about smacking upside the head.

"I can't tell if I wanna go home yet," I said to him. "You know what I mean? I'm just in one of those phases or moods where I don't know what I want, or what would make me feel better."

"Yeah, I get that. It's not like this is a normal situation. I would be surprised if you did know what would make you feel better."

We both chuckled, and I really couldn't tell you why. It wasn't funny, but it wasn't a real laugh either. I felt like I was watching a stupid Steve Harvey video that someone thought was funny and I was just trying to not be rude.

"You know what?" I said. "I don't know what's gonna happen in the next few days. I'll probably just stay in my room, in the dark, doing nothing. But next week maybe, we should plan something fun like go on a hike and watch a lot of movies, and then after the day is done we can go to the cemetery and tell Veena all about it."

Jack looked at me like I got a perfect score on a test and actually cared for once.

"Let's do it," Jack held out his hand, but not for a handshake, for *our* handshake. Two pats on the palm, a slide down each other's forearms, and the least sassy snaps in the history of finger snapping. Veena always used to tease us about it. I liked to think she was just jealous of our awesomeness.

The two of us waited around for what felt like hours, but I think it was only about fifty minutes. I didn't want to ask either of my parents to leave their own daughter's funeral, so I impatiently sat around until my grandfather offered to drive Jack and I home. The drive was completely silent, which was probably the wrong choice, but I thought we'd done enough crying for one day.

Jack stayed for a few more hours until his mom wanted him home. Kendra was always way more over protective of Jack than my mom was with Veena and I, and I knew my sister's accident wasn't gonna help with that situation.

That night, I might have slept for an hour and a half. Thank God. I was barely sleeping twenty minutes the last six nights. And I probably would have slept even longer if the stupid phone hadn't rung at nine in the morning.

My mom opened my door by saying, "Knock, knock." She had this thing about knocking where she didn't actually do it.

"Wha-" I mumbled, not yet conscious.

"Look, honey -" I immediately hated the sound of her voice and those words. The last time she said that to me was a week before when she told me my sister was gone. "You don't have to do this, but the police want to ask you a few questions, and they want you to come to the station whenever you can today."

The police station?

"Why? What do they need me for?" I guess I didn't need to sound too mockingly defensive, but it was a genuine question.

"I'm not sure, baby, but that's why you don't have to go if you don't want to. I know, I...I don't know how much help you'll be."

These were usually the times when I asked Veena what to do. Not that it was a big deal. What were those cops gonna do? Arrest me for answering questions? Nah. But that's probably just what Veena would say.

"It's fine, I'll go. I wanna help if I can. Can you drive me?"

It felt so strange asking her that. I NEVER asked my mom to drive me places, unless it was absolutely necessary. Veena drove me everywhere. She loved driving and she actually cared about not burdening my mom with the duty of driving her child places they needed to go.

"Sure. Let me just get my keys."

My shoulders slowly lifted to my ears, and if my mind wasn't playing tricks on me, I swear they were also shaking. Why was I nervous? I guess cops just freaked me out. Being five feet tall around a whole bunch of large white guys with beer bellies was just...odd.

Lucky for my AHwhatever, (That's what I called my ADHD, because when I was little, and was first diagnosed, I was also hella dyslexic and gave up on things really easily.) the police station was only a few minutes away like everything else in this town. What didn't help my issues was running into the ugliest green car with a mark on it that looked like Thor's hammer scraped across it. I was looking at my feet like I usually did when my knee hit the headlight, but it was like getting your sweater caught on a door handle. Always when you're in a bad mood.

The police station smelled like tuna, and I freaking hate tuna. Lieutenant Barry, who was an odd, bald man with a mustache like every cop in the movies, introduced himself and walked us through the hallway. But after only a few steps inside, did I feel a swipe of dagger eyes poking at me and my mom as we walked through everyone. They all probably knew who I was. Essex, Connecticut was a small town, and things like this never happened. The captain, or chief or whoever she was probably noticed they were all staring since she subtly shoved them all away with a manila envelope.

"Nova Rosa?" She asked. She was a tall woman who definitely spent too much time ironing her suits, and wore her dark brown hair in a tight bun.

"Yes," my mom answered before I could.

"And your mother, Charlotte Rosa?"

"Yes," my mom answered, once again.

"I'm Captain Sanders." She reached out her hand and I shook it. Something about the way she did it made me appreciate that she didn't lean down and raise her voice to reflect my age and height. No. It was firm with little emotion. "I'm so sorry for your loss. You can come right this way. Thank you, Lieutenant." The captain nodded to Lieutenant Barry with more exaggeration than needed, and with the same forceful body language she gestured to the hallway and said to us, "We can go into my office."

We followed her for probably only twenty seconds. In my mind I kept going over what she was gonna ask me. Maybe I *did* do something wrong. Did I break her car somehow? Did they think I was the one who hit her? Okay, no that was stupid. I didn't have a permit or license. Man, I really needed more sleep.

"Right in here." Captain Sanders held the door open for us, welcoming us into a surprisingly slick, decorated office. Not that I ever pictured what a policewoman's office would ever look like, but if I ever were to do so, this wouldn't be it. I was too busy admiring the seventies, emo portraits of young guitarists to even notice there was already another detective in the room.

He was tall and handsome in a Timothée Chalamet kind of way; thin and dorky. But what really caught my eye was his slouch and catastrophic way of handling the pile of files in his arms. They looked like they were about to fly everywhere, and not gonna lie, I would have loved to see that.

"Hello," he finally said. "I'm Detective Baron. I'm the head investigator on Miss Rosa's case." Clearly, he was too occupied to shake anyone's hand.

Nobody said anything after that, including Detective Sanders. She was busy ruffling through her neatly stacked files on her desk. I couldn't imagine what was possibly going on in this town that required that much reporting. The town consisted of what...six thousand people?

"Do you have any more information?" My mom finally broke the silence. "Or any new evidence?"

"Mrs. Rosa, I was hoping your daughter could give us some more information."

I nodded my head and waited patiently for her to reinitiate the conversation, but I guess it took her a second to realize she needed to ask the questions. Was she expecting me to just blurt out my sister's whole life story?

"Miss Nova," she finally said. That was painful. "You were the last person to see your sister before she entered her car, correct?"

I remembered telling them that when we initially had to go to the morgue and identify my sister's body. Man, just thinking of the words "her body" was disturbing beyond description. I never got why people said that. It was her, it was Veena, not just a bunch of cells and organs.

"Do you remember anything out of the ordinary?" Sanders continued. "Was she in maybe a particularly odd mood?"

Why in the hell was that important?

"Um...I didn't notice. She was just going to work, like usual. She worked at this local coffee shop. I'm sorry, I don't understand why you think this is important."

"It's just routine," Detective Baron commented. For some reason, Captain Sanders leaned over her shoulder to shoot him a look that told him to shut up. *She* was the one running this thing.

"I would rather you have an actual answer than just...whatever that answer was."

My mom was still, after fifteen years, always shocked with my constant tone; icy, and unfiltered.

"Nova," she whispered.

"What? You already confirmed it was a hit and run. Why else would the person responsible leave the scene of the crime? It was their fault and you're trying to blame my sister, aren't you?"

Captain Sanders was clearly used to people speaking to her like this. A woman in a powerful position? Damn. She must have had to shut down shit faster than a rated R movie at a twelve year old's sleepover. Although, the fact that she seemed used to people complaining about how they did their jobs, made me nervous.

"We are simply trying to look at this case from every angle so we don't miss a single thing." Sanders put her hands together in a prayer position and bobbed them forward and back with every other syllable, as if she were trying to lecture me.

"Is this what you say to rape victims?" I asked without raising my voice by a single notch.

"NOVA!" Even though my mom did.

"Anything you tell us will help us figure out who is responsible for this," said Detective Baron, backing up into the wall. I'm not sure who he was afraid of; the five foot, black and purple haired emo girl, with eyeliner that made her look like a raccoon, or the crying mother that could suddenly snap like a turtle whenever her teenage daughter acted like a goddamn teenager. Shocker right? What a twist.

"If you have any useful questions for me, let me know." I stood up and grabbed my mother by the arm and pulled her up with me. "But just because I am clearly so polite, I will reassure you, my sister wasn't angry driving, she wasn't changing the music on her phone, she wasn't under the influence, and she wasn't tired. She was the best driver I'd ever driven with, and she was never in a bad mood. She was never late, she always got straight A's, and her dream was to graduate a semester early and go to Princeton. She was overly responsible, if you will. That's the type of person she was, and you should probably write that down 'cause clearly you forget common protocols."

Now, this was different for the two police officers. A fifteen-year-old girl refusing to be manipulated by authority? Please.

With my hand still wrapped around my mother's forearm I stormed out of the office and I walked so fast I almost forgot which way to go. Luckily, by the time I was out of sight from the office window I was able to ask for directions without feeling a sense of defeat.

"You can let go of my arm now, Nova." Honestly, I didn't even realize it was still there, but I brushed off her shirt as I took my hand away and immediately went back to outrageous aggression.

"I'm sorry all of the cops in this god-for-saken town are twats, Mom."

My surprise by the fact she didn't yell at me for using that word lingered for the rest of our conversation.

"They're just trying to do their jobs, sweetheart."

I could tell she didn't truly believe that. She was just making excuses. Plus, she knew they were the only people who had real authority to find out who hit Veena.

Right before we were about to exit the failed tragedy known as the police department, I stopped in front of my mother, firmly planted my feet into the cracked concrete floor and said, "Look, Mom. If I hadn't said that to them, they would be steering themselves in the wrong direction. We both know that. Veena would never drive if she knew she couldn't, and she would never even touch her phone while her foot was on the gas pedal. There was no way this was her fault." Something shifted in my mom's eyes. There was a little bit of comfort that lifted from deep within her stomach, to her mind and soul. She knew I was right. She just needed me to confirm it for her first. "And besides, it's not like they're gonna stop trying to find out what happened just because I gave them a crash course on how to do their jobs. Technically they work for us."

Just by a hair, she lifted one corner of her mouth. It wasn't a real smile. I had gotten real familiar with what those looked like the past few days, but it was the closest she'd gotten in what felt like a really long time.

"Why don't I take you out to dinner at Veena's favorite place?" I asked her. "Let's stay in tonight, but tomorrow? We can order her favorite pancakes?" I knew my mother also loved those blueberry pancakes. My mouth watered just thinking about them.

"I think that's a wonderful idea, baby. I think she'd really like that."

The rest of the night was filled with nothing but anxiety. Even before my sister died, I would constantly have these weird, yet somehow boring panic fights. Not exactly attacks, but my brain and I would certainly have our disagreements and altercations.

Sometimes I couldn't do anything but sit in my room and stare at myself in the mirror. I didn't necessarily over think my looks, presence, or body weight, but my general self-worth? I would constantly play every awkward or distressing interaction in my head over and over again, and tonight, my memory offered me exclusive invitations to rehash all the bad encounters I ever had with my sister.

One night when we were young, I got so mad at her for taking a few of my stickers for a school project that I hit her. Hard, and in the face. Now, remember this; Veena only hit me when she was a toddler who thought that was the only form of communication. But the look on her face when she realized I would hit her over stickers, I'll never forget it. She was only maybe twelve, but she felt betrayed. We'd been so close, and I guess I wasn't smart enough to express my anger in another way. There were some things that I'll never get to fix.

Again, like almost every other night this past week, I only got about forty-five minutes of sleep. I woke up knowing immediately what would make me feel better; a walk in the woods, down the street from my mother's house. I almost always went alone. I preferred it that way, but whenever Veena needed me, or wanted to cheer me up, she knew where to find or bring me. About a quarter of a mile into the woods stood a small bridge. It had to have been at least forty years old. Don't get me wrong, it was sturdy as far as I knew. About a foot deep of two by fours were all nailed on top of each other to make the slightly rounded, ten-foot-long, and four feet wide bridge.

The railings broke off long ago. Honestly, I don't even remember them. I think my first memory on that bridge was standing right smack in the middle and feeling afraid that I was going to fall. So instead, I sat down to throw the pebbles into the small stream. Why was I throwing pebbles into a sad little river and calling it entertainment? I sure do hope I never learn the answer to that question, but that was still when it had a stream. It dried out years ago. I remember seeing the waterless bridge for the first time after winter and crying that it had gone away. I brought Veena to see, and she told me we could grab buckets and make the stream ourselves. I immediately felt better because I was way too lazy to do any of that crap myself.

When I finally arrived at the bridge, I hopped onto the top, sat down and dangled my feet. After just a few minutes my back started to hurt. My mother never lets me forget how terrible my posture still is, but I must have stared at the ground where the stream used to be for at least a half an hour. Something about it was peaceful, but still I couldn't stop thinking, and this was usually my place where I *didn't* think.

Oddly enough, I wasn't thinking about Veena precisely. I was thinking about my parents. I guess it wasn't *that* odd, but I couldn't help but wonder what it would have been like if I was the one taken instead of Veena. She would have taken care of them way better than me. I didn't think I was doing the best job so far. They would have been her top priority for the rest of her life. She would have made it her full-time job to make sure they were okay. Luckily, after a while, I was able to brush those thoughts out of my mind, and just...exist.

I ended up losing track of time, but it felt good. By this time next year, I was going to be sixteen, and there was no way my mother wouldn't force me to get a summer job. I was supposed to be spending basically my last summer of freedom with my sister, and this was as close as I was gonna get. This was the only type of enjoyment that I could possibly endure; being by myself.

My back hadn't felt that stiff in a while. When I stretched and rolled my shoulders up and back, I noticed something that strangely drew my attention. Normally a deer wouldn't catch my eye like it did in that moment. Seeing deer in New England is like seeing a drunk middle-aged man at a Red Sox game; often and ordinary but they're still gonna catch your attention, but this one looked straight into the bullseye of my forehead. I could have sworn it looked at me like it wanted to ask me the world's most complex and petrifying questions.

My feet still dangled off the bridge. They still rocked in circles, from side to side. They were basically on autopilot by now. But as my eye contact with this deer lingered, it was like my feet grew a mind of their own. Suddenly, they had an urge to jump down five feet to the ground, and for some reason my arms wanted to join in. They sure did have quite a sense of humor.

I felt my butt scrape against the rotting wood right before my heavy legs pulled me down to the barren stream. If it was concrete that my feet were colliding with, I probably would have broken an ankle or two, but it was squishy, soft mush with ingredients such as wet leaves, dry grass, and tiny little tree branches. My legs landed in the most heroic Wonder Woman pose I'd ever landed in. My back knee almost touched the ground but somehow my strength overpowered my drop. I would have felt cooler about my badass stance, but I needed to remind myself I was only pushed off a puny little bridge that was, at this point, maybe six inches above my head. It really wasn't that cool.

I propped myself back up to see the strangest thing; the deer was still there, and it was still staring straight at me, except now, it seemed like it was seeing through my soul. Not *into* my soul, *through* my soul, like I was completely transparent. The hypnotizing interaction was distracting enough for me to take a moment to realize I had cut the palm of my hand. Just a small incision from pushing myself off the splinter infested bridge. It didn't hurt per se, but I wiped the single drop of blood off on my black pants.

It was only a second that I had my head down, but when I looked up the deer was walking toward me. Still gazing into my eyes, but she was moving. I felt no harm coming my way. Like I said, deer were all around this town. Deer never hurt people, but the conscience that my legs developed grew fear and began to walk backwards, under the bridge. Steady, and silent. My left foot stepped into the shade under the bridge and the moment my right foot met with the other, a shiver exploded from my shoulder. Almost like a cold rush, but not quite. It was more like a tension relief, but it felt more magical than medical. At the same time, the most refreshing, cool wind brushed across my face. None of this resembled being in a dream. It was as if I was waking up from a dream. The chill made goosebumps pop all over my skin, but in a pleasant way, like the earth was giving me a gentle greeting. The birds seemed happy to see me too. The chirps were on a higher pitch and much brighter, or at least this environment forced me to acknowledge them for once.

On the other side of the bridge the sun beamed a more golden light, and I promise with every fiber of my being, there were sparkles in the air. They shimmered through the sky and the woods like the scales of a mermaid. Naturally, my eyes closed adjusting to the light, but when I opened them back up, the deer was gone. It made sense, deer were quiet and quick. I didn't think much of it.

Something about the entire afternoon gave me the creeps, or maybe it was just the sudden need to do something different. The world seemed to be moving slower, and my bed called out to me, but I took the long path out of the woods. After continuing along the dried-up stream, and kicking a few wet leaves out of my pathway, I thought I should check on my cut, but when I eyed my palm, the only thing there was my birthmark shaped like a demented star. There was no evidence of any scrape. No blood, no splinter. I checked my other hand just to be sure I wasn't stupid, but still nothing. Wouldn't be the first time I imagined an injury. Hypochondria was my best frenemy.

The rest of the walk in the woods felt numb. I kept playing *Old Town Road* in my head, but I had no idea what my body was doing, including my eyes. If there was a dragon sleeping in the woods right in front of me, I wouldn't have remembered or noticed.

Finally I came to the edge of the woods. The edge of the sidewalk was in sight, and right as I could acknowledge what my fingers and toes were up to, I saw feet walking along the sidewalk. God, I swore to myself that if it was someone I knew, I would have run away pretending I was jogging even though I was wearing converse and jeans.

I kept my head down like always, but in the corner of my eye, I saw the feet turn around and whoever those feet belonged to immediately yelled out, "There you are. I knew you'd be in here."

The shock started in my ears, then it traveled all the way down my spine and into my appendages. I knew that voice, and it made me terrified to look up. But this voice kept talking.

"What did you see a bear in there or something?" The voice laughed. I knew that laugh too.

My eyes stretched wide as I slowly looked up and locked eyes with another pair of eyes I never thought I'd see again.

"*Veena*?"

PART 2: JULY 20TH, 8:47AM

"Veena."

I couldn't stop saying her name as I carefully walked over to her. The last thing that I wanted was to walk too fast and have her drift away into a black hole or something.

"Veena, I -"

"What's wrong?" Veena asked as she gave me a look that hinted she was about to fight someone. "Is that bitch, Brittany, back at you again?"

Brittany Cavalry was my childhood bully that probably forgot I existed, and I also forgot she existed until that moment.

"What? No! I just -"

A few things; One...I couldn't finish my sentences. Two...I couldn't feel my toes so I kept tripping over them, so she probably thought I was drunk. And three...What was I supposed to ask her?

Was I in a magical or fake world that still had her in it? Where the hell was I? Did I die too? Oh shit...DID I DIE TOO?

"What's going on?" I didn't realize how much the volume of my voice skyrocketed until after I screamed into my hands.

"Okay, alright. Let's get you home." Veena put her arms around me and we began to walk. Even though I was shaking beyond control, the warmth and comfort pouring out of my sister's body was like lightning, but if the lightning was made of daisies and roses. I never thought I would get to feel her touch ever again, and it just made me shake even harder. "Come on. Everything's okay. We can talk about it when we are nice and warm in bed with a root beer float."

I was nearly silent the rest of the way home. My breathing slowed down, but I still had trouble expanding my diaphragm enough to breathe comfortably and without making disturbing throat noises. She probably thought a frog was following us the whole time.

Before I knew it, I had a giant root beer float in my hand and I was propped up on my bed. Veena turned on my T.V. and put on *Game of Thrones*. I wasn't technically allowed to watch that show so Veena put her index finger to her lips and turned the volume down.

"So, what's going on?" She asked. I forgot that I was gonna need to come up with an answer for that, so I just said the first thing that came to my mind.

"I fell asleep in the woods and had a bad dream." I didn't want to see her reaction to that crap of a story, so I chugged down a big sip of my drink.

"What?" She laughed. "Why did you fall asleep in the woods?"

Good question. Two options for a response came to my mind; I was sleepwalking, or I was depressed from getting a bad grade on a test. No way she was buying the second one, so sleepwalking it was.

"I guess I just dozed off and wandered into the woods." That seemed like a good enough response that would confuse her and tire her out too much to ask any more questions.

"Alright," she said, taking a deep breath and shrugging her shoulders. "But how do you feel now? You good?"

"Yeah," I lied, or did I? I still wasn't sure, because if this reality was some sort of cruel joke just to watch my sister die all over again, it wasn't funny. "Can I ask you something though?"

"You know you always can." Man, I missed that genuine consoling smile. It was something only an older sister could have.

"Has there been anything weird going on lately? Are Mom and Ralph okay? Is Dad okay?"

"Well, if you're talking about Dad's horrible date last week, then I'm not sure how to answer that. I thought he really liked her, but oh well."

I only really heard the first part of that answer, and then I had a puzzling thought. What day was it here? Was it the same as my world or whatever I was supposed to call it? Veena must have thought I had really lost it when I booked it over to the other side of my room to look at my calendar.

Saturday, July 20th, 2019.

It was the same day as my world. So, I guess, it was just...a parallel universe.

I audibly laughed at the silent sound of "parallel universe" in my head. Now *I* knew that I was losing it. Wow.

"I'm sorry," I said as a single happy tear ran down my cheek. "I really am fine, I promise. I'm just really happy to see you."

Veena didn't bother asking why I was so overwhelmed to see her even though I probably saw her a few hours ago or something like that. Unless...

Oh shit, I almost said out loud. *What if there's another me* in this universe? *What if I run into her and there's two of us?*

After a breath or two, I realized that, once again, all I was doing was overthinking. My sister was here. What else could I want? That's all I'd been asking for; to see her again. But she didn't know that, because wherever the hell we were, the accident never happened.

"Did I make that root beer float alright?" Veena asked, breaking my AHwhatever.

"You always make it perfect. Who do you think you are? Mom?" I wiped away a few tears as I tried to pull myself into a few seconds of laughter once again.

"Hey! Give her some credit, she at least tries."

I took another sip of my drink, but it was hard. My lungs burned as my chest tightened, and my throat felt like it was about to close. Great. I welcomed with tightly closed arms, a freaking panic attack.

"Hey, hey, hey," I barely heard Veena say. She took the drink out of my hand and put her hands on my shoulder. It took me a second to realize she was trying to get me to lay down.

As my head hit the pillow, I had a change of heart. There was no way that I was about to fall asleep now. No. Veena was here. Every moment needed to be embraced and thoroughly lived. My body stayed spread along my duvet, but I made it apparent that my eyes were gonna stay wide open.

"How have you been this past week?" I asked without thinking about it first.

"Why do you ask about this past week?" she laughed. "You know you've seen me every day this past week, right?"

"I have?"

Oops. Didn't mean to ask that.

"Yeah, silly."

"Right. Sorry. Guess this was just a bad week for my depression. It makes me forget things. I guess I just really want you to talk. Talk to me about anything."

I'd heard people say that in movies. Me not being much of a talker and a terrible listener, I never thought that would be appealing, but in that moment, I almost pulled out my phone and started to record her.

Veena talked to me for hours. At least I think it was hours. Most of the time she just complained about her ex-boyfriend, Brian. I always liked him, but he was the dumbest human being I'd ever met and was a terrible match for Veena. Nonetheless, she talked about their year-and-a-half relationship and how he, once again, wanted to get back together. Something about how they were gonna be "walking down the same roads". Even though Veena was probably going to an Ivy League school a semester early while Brian's grade point average was no more than 2.0. That boy couldn't navigate a Cheesecake Factory menu, let alone a college application.

The only other topic of the night was about Raya, Veena's best friend from birth, and my biggest enemy. Or should I say, I was *her* biggest enemy. When I was little, I did absolutely nothing to her, but she made it her life's mission to torture me like I was a spy in the C.I.A.

One time, when I was eight, this demon with lipstick dared me to slide down the big kid's slide on the playground that was shaped like a dragon. I didn't want to because of my reasonable fear of being scared. But she basically dragged me up there and shoved me down, and you know what I did? You know what my eight-year-old body did? Not three-year-old, eight-year-old. I peed my freaking pants, and she screamed about it all the way home.

Veena was only ten, and she consoled me while I walked with soiled pants, but did Raya get any reprimandation? Hell no. And also, I'm aware that that's not a real word, but I used it a lot as a kid when I was complaining about her.

Now, apparently the past few weeks, Raya had also been having boy troubles. This boy man person whose name I do not care about had broken things off with Raya. Here was the kicker and my favorite part; he'd asked out Veena a minimum of three times before he told Raya that he was kind of interested in her. Damn! Something about that was so satisfying to listen to, and absolutely hilarious.

Everything felt normal. There was no pain. No more tears after talking for a while.

"Are you hungry?" Veena asked after looking at the clock. "It's dinner time, you wanna go to Bernie's?"

"Absolutely. Let's get outta here."

We continued to talk with our normal sister bond as we walked down the street in the twilight sky, but the second we approached the diner, my feet glued to the pavement.

"What is it?" Veena asked, or at least I think she did.

"I'm supposed to meet -" I was supposed to meet Mom at this diner, but not here. She was probably waiting for me right then, but I couldn't tell Veena that I had to cross under a magical bridge and then come back. "I'm sorry, Veena. I gotta go. I'll explain later."

"Oh, okay. Yeah, no worries."

I really didn't want to leave, but I knew I wouldn't be able to stay away. I squeezed her hand for way too long, and waited until the last minute before I let go. I can't explain it, but I knew I was gonna see her again.

I ran as fast as I could back to the bridge. Still, I wasn't one hundred percent sure it was going to work, but what other ideas did I have to supernaturally return to my world? I was never that creative.

After almost tripping over a few tree branches, I finally reached the bridge. Ice struck my nerves. What if it was gonna hurt? What if it was gonna alter my D.N.A. like in the movies? Man, I really needed to stop watching the C.W. channel.

In my line of sight, I saw the spot where the mysterious deer stood. For some reason, thinking about that deer gave me comfort, like I knew her from somewhere, and we'd developed a special relationship.

Thinking about my mom waiting there at Bernie's, worried about where I was helped me push myself to walk back under the bridge. All I needed was that little push. I counted down, "Three, two, one," and just like that, I felt the relief from my shoulders beaming through the sunlight once again, and I was back in my own world.

There was no time to think about my sister feeling so far away. My mother was waiting, and the last thing I needed was for her to think her now only child was in trouble.

My feet felt like little birds flying across the sidewalk. The light, hovering feeling was liberating. This was anything but the appropriate time to be thinking about this, but I'd always liked running. Besides reading a ton of anime, it was the only thing that was kind of a hobby.

The beasts could have kept pumping, but I saw my mother waiting outside the diner on her phone and I slowed down as I approached her.

"Young lady!" she screamed. "You had me worried sick!" The last and only time she'd ever hugged me that tightly was when we got the news about Veena.

"I'm sorry, I'm sorry. I got caught up in something. Guess my phone died. I pulled it out of my pocket to see if I was right. I was. Dumbass. As I tried to open my phone, I noticed that once again, my hand was bleeding. And unfortunately, my mom noticed too.

"Oh, honey. Let's go inside and clean that up."

As she aggressively grabbed my hand to pull me inside whether I liked it or not, I couldn't help but think. A few minutes ago, I was in the same place with my sister, or a different version of my sister. It was just...something else. We were so happy a few minutes before, and then suddenly, my mom and I were completely different people in this timeline. I couldn't tell her about the other world, I could *never*. She'd think I was crazy, or even worse, she might believe me.

Our usual waitress, Lauren, sat us down at our usual table. Lauren had been there forever, and she loved it. Although, she hadn't seen us since the accident. I was curious as to what she was gonna say.

"Charlotte, Nova," she began, "It's lovely to see you." Her eyes grew glossier with every breath. She didn't know what to say. I could just tell.

"It's lovely to see you too," I said, so my mother wouldn't have to.

"How – I mean – " Lauren couldn't finish.

To my surprise, my mother gently grabbed Lauren's hand, grew a shaky smile and said, "Thank you." It was more of a whisper, but the power was soul piercing.

They exchanged caring smiles before Lauren broke the silence and said, "I'm going to miss her."

"She's going to miss you too."

I know this was a terrible thing to think, but I didn't know my mother was this strong. She'd understandably been so quiet that week, and she wasn't always the best at giving advice. But when it came to her daughters, she always knew what to say.

"Should I bring you the usual?" Lauren asked.

"Veena's usual actually. For the both of us. I think we'll be having that a lot in the future."

"Coming right up."

Until our pancakes and milkshakes came out, we sat in almost complete silence. I couldn't stop thinking about this other place, and I could tell my mom wasn't really ready to talk. Neither of us seemed to mind. She just needed my constant company, and I had already come to terms with that last week.

"Do you think you're gonna be up for going to school in the fall?" Mom asked as I bit into my pancakes. I looked at her like she was crazy, which was, of course, the extremely wrong decision.

"Yeah, of course. Veena would slap me upside the head."

"Right." She took a big gulp of her milkshake, which I was beyond happy to see. Sometimes I hated how good of a memory I have, but I noticed that pretty much none of the food in the cabinets or fridge had been touched for a while. It might not have had any nutrition, but still. Progress.

"We don't have to stay here for too long, Mom. I know we usually hang out and all afterwards, but I know you probably wanna go and lay down."

"I don't know yet. Maybe." She shrugged her shoulders and started picking her nails. The last time she picked her nails was when our dog Fufu died, three years ago. But in general, it was a sign that she was simply anxious, and didn't know what to do next, even if it was just standing up from a chair.

"You know, Ralph could have come. I wouldn't have cared," I told her, trying to change the subject.

"No, it's alright. He's done enough for me since I haven't been at work. I don't wanna drive him crazy."

"You? Drive *him* crazy?" And just like that, her smile cracked a little further than the last one.

"Hey, he's gotten better at, you know, closing doors...and stuff."

In general, it was unusual for me to joke like this with her. That was never the type of relationship we had. That was more of Veena's thing.

"Anything else you can think of?" I poked at her trying to get her to admit that Ralph was an oblivious slob, but we loved him anyway.

"I'll get back to you on that."

There was no noise that came from her laughter. Usually she had a ridiculous snort that Veena was always best at imitating. It was gonna be a long time before any of us heard that again, but there was something in my mother's eyes that told me she'd made peace with that, and it would return when she was ready.

Ralph picked us up from the diner since it was already pitch black out. By now, I was so anxious to get home, I was physically unable to stop drumming on the back of the passenger's seat. Gotta love that AHwhatever. Thankfully, I was about sixty three percent sure my mom didn't notice.

When I got upstairs, I was in one of those moods where I needed my room to be spit spot clean in order to do anything. No distractions. I couldn't afford any this time.

The night sky grew darker, and more layers gradually wrapped around my body. Eventually, I was in a tight, closed knit hoodie with only a small visible circle of my face. After I was a hundred and ten percent positive that my parents were asleep, I pulled out my laptop and started searching for everything that had to do with the words, "magic", or "supernatural" in it. I swear I scanned through at least twenty articles that had to do with the television show *Supernatural* just to make certain I didn't miss anything. But after a while I felt like a broken record. Just reading the same crap over and over again.

A few articles were from a few psychics that claimed they could "enter another world", but I've never believed a single thing that any so-called "psychic" has ever said and I don't plan on doing so. But if I'm being real, I don't usually believe anything that the internet says. So, what the hell was I doing in this mindless blackhole?

No. I needed authentic, raw evidence as to what could be happening here, and the only place I was gonna get that from was right next door; Veena's room.

"I'm going straight to Hell for this," I whispered to myself, even though that was the very last place I believed in.

I looked at the clock; twelve thirty. Still a hundred and ten percent certain the parents were still asleep or at least wouldn't get up. Nevertheless, I was still paranoid, and for other reasons, nervous. Veena's room had been off limits for me emotionally. The first few days after she died I held my hand up to my eyes when I passed her door to get to mine. It was instinctual. When I walked up the stairs the first time, I just did it automatically. I couldn't bear to look.

Now, I knew I needed to try. This could lead to answers. Answers about anything and everything. Was she a witch? *Woooow*...glad I didn't say that shit out loud.

The hallway was pitch black, which meant I had to close my door in case burglars were casually walking around the house and I needed to be able to hear them entering my room. My phone's flashlight poured over my sister's door and my first instinct was to once again cover my eyes, but I resisted. It was hard, but empowering, and it felt amazing. Guess I was stronger than I looked.

Before I knew it, I was in Veena's room and the light switch was on. I stood in the middle of her pink, flower rug and turned in circles. And after a few turns, I arrived at the conclusion that I had no clue what I was looking for.

"Why am I so stupid?" I asked myself for some strange reason.

The desk. The desk was a good place to start. That's what they all did in the movies. No specific examples came to mind, but whatever.

The drawers were filled with crap, which was surprising since you could literally eat off Veena's floor. She was the tidiest person I knew.

Nothing seemed of extreme value. Mainly just receipts, pieces of scrap paper, and old gum stacked on top of one another in this 10x12x8 drawer. But if Veena was hiding anything she wouldn't put it in such an obvious place. Under the bed? Still too obvious. No, she would definitely hide it behind something where only her dainty hands could reach. My hands were rather manly, but I was still a fifteen-year-old girl. I could make it work.

Nothing behind the desk, nothing behind the bureau, but there was still one place I'd barely even looked at; the vanity.

Man, that girl loved make-up and hair. *Of course* she would hide something in her three-hundred-dollar vintage vanity. It didn't take long for me to notice there was nothing behind or under it. So just to be extra sure, I checked the single drawer that was apparently exclusively reserved for lipstick that looked way too expensive for Veena's barista paycheck. Nothing. Where else was I supposed to look?

I dramatically closed the drawer in frustration, but as I sliced the brown, polished wood away from me, I felt something, some sort of resistance. Like the top of the drawer got caught on something.

"Ah - haaaaahhh," I barely whispered to myself. My middle finger clung onto the spiral of a pocket-sized notebook and I pulled it down from the top of the drawer to hear the sound of velcro tearing apart. Man, this girl took every precaution except for her sister being a total genius.

The cover of the journal had the ugliest pink and purple flowers on it with cheap glitter smothering them. I flipped that shit over real fast.

On the first page, my eyes were immediately drawn to the date. Except not only was it a date, it had the time too. Odd.

Nov 11th, 2018, 4:06pm

> Brian basically threatened me
> again. "I'm blocking you on
> Facebook just so you know." He
> seriously thinks that I owe him
> something, and I'm honestly kind
> of scared of him. I wasn't even
> allowed to look at another guy
> when I was with him.

What? She never told me about this. I knew Brian was kind
of a waste of space, but I was wrong. He could possibly be smarter
than I thought, but a hell of a lot more abusive.

Jan 3rd, 2019, 9:32pm

> And once again Brian yelled at
> me when I took a sip of his coffee
> that I bought for him. "Get your
> own." Literally his exact words.
> We're not even together any
> more. I was just trying to be nice.

For a moment, just a moment, I was hurt that she never
even gave me a hint that this was happening. But quickly I came to
my senses that I was being selfish and insensitive. This wasn't
about me, and she was probably embarrassed. I flipped through
every single page that was filled. All of the entries were about
Brian.

Holy shit. This wasn't a journal, this was insurance in case
Brian ever went too far. She was probably just trying to stay civil
with him because she didn't want things to get worse. Clearly, she
was terrified of him. Originally, I was looking for answers about
why she existed in an alternate universe, but this could be useful in
another situation.

Creeeeeak, I heard coming from the hallway. Great. Either
it was a burglar like I always thought it was, or it was a nosy parent.
Either way, they could see that Veena's light was on and I needed
to hide the journal. Actually, I didn't know why I would need to
hide it from a burglar, but I threw it back into the vanity drawer

anyways.

"Hey," my mom said as she was opening up the door. Her eyes were puffier than normal. She probably cried herself to sleep for longer than usual.

"Hey. What are you doing up?" I tried to look as normal as I could just randomly sitting at Veena's vanity. I had the feeling that most grieving siblings would lay in the middle of the floor or on the bed, but my mother knew I was different a while ago.

"I had to go to the bathroom. What are you doing in here?" She was about to cry again looking in Veena's room. Without a doubt, she knew she wasn't doing it, but her eyes darted around the room as if she hadn't looked at it in a hundred years. If only I could tell her, *"Veena's out there. I don't know if it's possible for you to see her, but I can, and she loves you. I swear, somewhere out there, she's alive."*

I jumped up out of the chair and ran to my mother's embrace. My sixth sense kicked in. I always knew when someone was in need of a hug, and I gave phenomenal hugs. The only non-emo thing about me.

Her shiver was intense, but normal. She wasn't that much taller than me, so her head fit in my shoulder perfectly.

"Mom, I'm not going anywhere. I swear, I'm always going to be here for you."

She lifted her head from my shoulder, gently cupped my face with her motherly instinctual care and said straight into my eyes, "You don't know that, baby."

My jaw tightened to the point of no wiggle room. What was I supposed to say to that? I mean she was right. Nobody ever knows what's going to happen tomorrow. So, my fingers and toes froze like my jaw, and I said absolutely nothing. Before I knew it, my mom walked back to her room and shut the door without saying anything else.

It took me another few moments to move like a conscious person again, but once I could feel my fatigued shoulders move freely, I took the journal back out of the drawer and went back into my room.

PART 3: JULY 22ND, 12:37AM

There was a small voice in the back of my head that told me I was gonna actually sleep that next night. Now, this voice gave me no guarantee that it was gonna be a good sleep, but from what I was getting from this surprisingly nasally voice, was that I was to be asleep for a hell of a lot longer than any night the previous week.

LIES.

My eyes hadn't been that wide open since after I watched *A Quiet Place* for the first time. And just like that movie, there was nothing but silence.

The construction workers down the street from my house finally finished whatever they were doing, and my mom finally went to bed without crying about not being able to say goodnight to Veena.

For me, my guess was that I didn't know where I was in the process of grief. My sister was still out there, whatever *there* was, and I didn't know why. The more I thought about it, the more I truly believed this other world was there for a reason. Specifically for me.

Deeper into the night, I went further and further into the most buried parts of my brain. I thought if there was another Nova in this other world, could she come into my world? I also wondered, if I were to change something about my appearance in this other world, would it stick in my world? But the thing that I couldn't stop worrying about was if I was able to return. Was this a one-time thing? Did I miss my only chance to truly say good-bye to my sister?

My eyes were so glued to the ceiling that I, no joke, noticed the change in brightness when the sun came up. At around five in the morning, I figured this was gonna be my only chance to get out of the house while my mom was still asleep, and she wouldn't ask all of these questions that made me want to scream, "I DON'T KNOW" at everything she asked.

It was warm enough outside that I took my usual route to exit my house; out of my bedroom window and down the vines. Usually when it was cold out, my fingers instantly froze when I touched the metal on my roof outside my window.

The vines were especially prickly climbing down, but no one was on the road to catch me being a rebel, so I took my goddamn time. As usual, my ankles did that weird tingly thing when I jumped from the vines to the grass, but I shook it off and sprinted my size six feet towards that bridge. I was gonna break my ankle soon. I could feel it.

The bridge seemed farther away than normal. Maybe my nerves were just distracting me, but putting my foot in front of the other came with unusual difficulty. What if I couldn't get back in? Man, I could be so thick. Why didn't I think about this before I left her in the first place?

The aching thought refused to escape from my head. But that wasn't the only thing stabbing my brain. What if I were to say goodbye knowing I'll never see her again? I didn't get to say good-bye to Veena in this world. She left for work in a hurry. I didn't even get an, "I'm leaving!" from her. But would I be able to leave her knowing it *was* goodbye? Would I be able to pull away?

My tired feet finally reached the bridge, but before I got even five feet away from it, before I even walked down into the ditch, I stopped. Frozen. Basic 101 on how my brain works; I don't like having unanswered questions. My brain always needs to know what's going on, or it will melt and swirl around in my head at the same time. What can I say? I'm nosy.

What was so special about this bridge? I guess it was symbolic in a way, but who was it that put this magical portal under it, or whatever it was. Now would have been a great time for Dumbledore to be real. Oh, damn...was Hogwarts real?!

Focus, idiot. Focus.

My feet couldn't move, and I mean that directly. Flashbacks of my middle school depression rushed back to me. One time in social studies class, the bell rang, signaling the end of class. I didn't hear it, and I didn't move, or more so *couldn't*. I couldn't even lift my chin to look at my teacher when she asked me what was wrong. Every cell in my body felt low and numb. My mom took me to the emergency room that afternoon.

Back then, I usually felt the most depressed after thinking too much about what I was going to have to do the rest of that day. It was common, random things like too much homework, too many chores and violin lessons. All of these events that I had to put physical effort into put a bad feeling in the pit of my stomach. Like I knew I was gonna mess it all up, and I knew I was gonna hate it for no reason at all.

In this moment, it was no different. Something was gonna go wrong, and it could be anything. But I knew one thing; saying goodbye to my sister again would destroy me. So instead of getting right to it and passing under the bridge, I sat my butt down in the dirt. Classic me, just sitting still.

Desperation filled my veins. I wanted to run right to my sister more than anything, but I couldn't. At least an hour went by when I realized my butt had gone numb, but I tried to pay no attention to it. My focus was more occupied with my dry eyes staring at that bridge.

Ever since I can remember, I always found the neutral, ruffling noises of the woods soothing. But not a meditative soothing. More like an awakening soothing. I could do homework here. I could draw here, or write in my journal with the sun spraying its rays onto my paper. This was the only thing that made me feel like I could embrace the strength to walk back under that bridge.

"I can do this," I said to myself. "I have the opportunity to see her again. I have to."

I tried not to slide too fast down the little ditch leading to where the stream used to be. No rain was to be seen in a while. The dirt was all too dry. All it truly did was get my heart racing the appropriate amount to lift my spirits and confidence. Just a little kick of adrenaline was helpful in ninety-nine percent of situations.

Like I said before, the bridge was ancient, and it didn't age like a fine wine like Dolly Parton. It was more like Keith Richards; many layers of roughness, but still somehow exquisite. After a moment of admiration, I once again noticed a force of power pulling me towards that scraggly arch of wood. I couldn't help but smile. Veena, she was out there, and the closer I got, the more I knew I was gonna be able to go through it again. On the other side was my sister's beautiful smiling face.

Only a few steps away now. I'm not stupid. So, I, of course, still proceeded with caution. Subconsciously, my fingertips reached out to touch whatever I was reaching for. The barrier had to be made out of some sort of entity that beamed with spirit. It was safe. I sensed it.

"Just a little closer," I could barely hear myself say. "It's okay. I can do this. Three more steps. Three...two -"

"Nova!"

Really?

I whipped my head around so fast I could barely see Jack standing a few feet above me at the top of the little hill. His sour and perplexed look told me he'd been standing there for at least a few seconds.

"What are you doing?" he asked, barely moving his overly stiff, pipe cleaner body.

"Nothing!" I responded way too quickly and even more loudly than I meant to. All these little thoughts ran through my head like ten different roller coasters trying to avoid each other. If I told Jack about any of this, even if I told him a hypothetical theory that this bridge could be haunted, he would write a novel about it after sending me to an asylum. He had such little faith in anything remotely supernatural, and he was less religious than I was. Believe me, *that* was hard to do.

"Have you been out here for a while?" Jack asked, coming to join me in the ditch.

"Kinda."

"Hm. I thought I would find you out here. I went to your mom's, and she wasn't too pleased to find out you weren't there."

Oh no. She was gonna rip my ear off literally and metaphorically later. That's what I get for turning off my phone and being an anti-social maniac.

"Don't worry," Jack defensively put up his hands before pulling out his phone. "I'll text her saying you're here."

"Thanks. Man, she hates it when I come out here alone."

"She's just worried about you." The sadness in his eyes. He hadn't stopped looking at me like that this past week and a half. It was starting to make me feel pathetic. As if I needed to be treated like a puppy dog, but what else was he supposed to do? He hadn't gone through anything like this before, and neither had I. We didn't know what we were supposed to do, but then I had an idea.

"Hey, can you do me a favor?" I asked him, still unsure of how I was gonna phrase the next question.

"Of course. Anything," he responded. He would always say that to me. Even before Veena died.

"Can you cross under this bridge?" I was really hoping he wasn't gonna ask why.

"Why?"

Damn it.

"I heard it was good luck, and I think I could really use some of that right now." Well that was truly the stupidest answer I could have possibly given him. He was more than well aware of how unsuperstitious I was.

"Umm, sure." With a puzzled and suspicious look still on his face, he turned around. What was he supposed to do? He did, after all, say he would do *anything* for me. But because he sometimes liked to do things in the most complicated way possible, he started to go around to the other side of the bridge and went under the wrong way.

"No, no, you gotta go under this way." Then, he just looked annoyed. I didn't blame him.

"I'm not even going to ask." That was also something he said to me a lot.

Quickly, he walked towards the bridge. I almost told him to slow down, but that was probably unnecessary. My eyes stayed wide open and attentive as he passed right under the old bridge to the other side. From what I could tell he felt nothing out of the ordinary, and when he turned around to look at me, he confirmed that to be true.

"Stay right there for a second," I told him, holding my hand up like a wimpy cop. "You can see me, right?" Okay, I really didn't need to ask that crap.

"Yes, Nova. I can see you. Are you okay?"

"I'm fine. Just one more question. Do you feel any different?"

"I feel a little more concerned about you than I did before." He wasn't always great at sarcasm.

"Oh shush. I'm fine. I'm just weird. Come back over here." And I waved him back over to me as if I were the most normal human being that ever walked the planet. "Did you need me for something specific?" I asked him a little too assertively than I meant to. "Or did you just wanna hang out?"

"Well, there is something I think you should see."

Expecting him to continue that sentence, I popped my chin forward, impatiently waiting. Instead, he pulled his phone back out again and showed me something I was not expecting.

"HIGH SCHOOL STUDENT ARRESTED FOR STALKING!" The headline screamed on the online news article from the local paper.

"Keep reading and - just keep reading." Man, I hated the way he said that. The chill, the ice. Unpleasant beyond comparison.

HIGH SCHOOL STUDENT
ARRESTED FOR STALKING!

Early this morning Brian Ruben, an 18-year-old junior at Valley Regional High School, was arrested by the Essex police on stalking allegations by classmate Alyssa Casley. According to Casley, Ruben stalked her last year towards the end of their sophomore year of high school and recently this year.

According to Captain Sanders, from the Essex Police Department, Casley set up a camera to document Ruben's actions of waiting outside of her house and at her place of employment for hours at a time.

"His obsession lasted for only a few months last year," Casley told the police, "so I didn't file any complaints, but then it started again."

Ruben is being detained, so he was unavailable for comment.

Police records allege that Ruben waited in his car for hours at her house and tailed her car on her way to a friend's house, although he never approached her directly.

Although a minor, Casley's parents granted permission to print her name.

"Are you kidding me?" I complained. "They're making it sound like he was arrested without cause, and she's being aggressive."

"Finish reading it," said Jack with that same, icy look on his face.

Ruben was also charged for another, more recent stalking charge on Friday, July 12th.

According to the police, Ruben has denied this charge because his car was in a repair shop on July 12th.

Everything in me, including my blood, froze.

"July 12th? Are they sure?" I asked. My voice cracked and shivered all at once.

Jack gave a little shrug before he said, "The same day of the accident. I asked around and even Alyssa admits she might have just gotten scared and mistook his car for someone else's. It was almost dark. She probably doesn't want to tell the police because she doesn't want to lose credibility."

I should've known. After reading what Veena really thought about Brian, of course, he should have been a suspect in her hit and run.

"She's scared out of her mind," Jack continued. "Maybe Veena was too."

"Okay, hold on." I slapped my hands on my head and gently massaged my temple. It didn't help in the slightest, but I needed to give my hands something to do. I told Jack about everything that I found in Veena's diary the night before. How it all *could* make sense, but I still had hesitations. "We gotta consider a few other things. Brain is anything but a smart human being. I know he's reckless and creepy, but he would be the last person that thought he could get away with hitting her on purpose. And besides, they had barely been talking the last few months. Did he even know where her job was?"

Jack didn't answer. He probably hadn't taken any of that into consideration yet, but honestly, I trusted his judgment more than mine.

"Is it common for stalkers to stalk more than one woman?" I asked, like the sheltered human being that I was.

"Definitely, and didn't you say that he was a terrible driver? Maybe he didn't do it on purpose, but what if he was following her and things went wrong?"

I didn't know the answer, but I couldn't rule him out. What frustrated me the most was that the police probably didn't know about this, and I most certainly couldn't rest until I knew they were taking it into consideration.

"I have to go to the police with this," I said to Jack as I ran past him. "Hey, um, can you actually tell my mom where I'm going?"

"She's not going to like it," he agreed in the most annoying way possible. "But wait. You really should go and get your sister's journal if you're going to accuse him. You're going to need as much evidence as possible. It's going to take a lot of convincing with those guys."

PART 4: JULY 23RD, 9:16AM

Before leaving for the station, I was, for once, smart. Sneakers. Running in comfortable, badass, ripped up, black sneakers was the best way to release my rage before entering the Captain's office in the Essex Police Station. No real anger was necessary yet, but I could feel it crawling up my skin.

The impression these idiot cops gave me the other day was not the calming or convincing one they could have given to me and my mother. I'm sure that they thought they were doing a good job, but I thought they were incompetent. My issue with cops didn't fully originate from my issues with authority. It also came from the fact that they think they get my respect from wearing a badge and carrying a gun. And don't even get me started on my goddamn issues with guns.

Anyway, if these so-called "serve the public" cops did have the idea that Veena could have been hit on purpose, and this kid was at least questioned, then I would reconsider the whole "screw the police" scenario. But no promises.

My legs didn't get tired until I ran up the high stack of steps leading up to the police station. But there was no time to rest. Brian could be on bail by now, and if I knew Brian, he was too stupid to know how bail worked. If he did, he would probably run away to Mexico thinking it was just a few miles down the road.

The station smelled worse than usual. The stench of concrete and sweat shot up into my sensitive nose which almost distracted me from seeing two officers right in front of me who I was about to physically run into.

"Excuse me," I politely said to them, resisting covering up my nose. "Is there someone who I could talk to about the Rosa hit-and-run case?"

"The what?" The taller one said. He had the most hideous mustache and awkward blonde hair that definitely didn't suit him. But somehow it was still better than the shorter one who, I kid you not, had a patchy goatee that looked like a balding rat.

"The Rosa case from about a week and a half ago." My judgmental ass assumed that neither of them would know much about it since they were police officers with uniforms and not detectives. And let me tell you, I was right.

"Little Miss, we have no idea what you're talking about," the shorter one said, laughing.

He heard me say hit-and-run, right? Or did that go into one ear with a one-way ticket out the other? Why did he think this was funny?

"Rickers, Smith," said a familiar voice. "I can take it from here."

It was the Detective that questioned me the other day. Crap. What was his name? I could only hope I was able to smoothly get away with not knowing.

"Yes, Siiiir...um?"

Nailed it.

"Miss Rosa. I'm sorry I can't remember your first name."

"Good, 'cause I can't remember yours." Usually I don't like to be borderline rude, but I felt like this guy would listen to me more if I was blunt with him.

"No worries," he almost laughed. "I'm Detective Baron, but call me Tom."

"Okay, Tom." And for a few brief seconds, I forgot that I was the one that came up to him and it was my turn to do the awkward talking. Instead of asking me what I was randomly here for, Tom just lifted his eyebrows and cocked his chin down.

"Oh, my bad, sorry. Um, I wanted to ask you about this."

I forgot that I still had my phone off, and the amount of times Tom scratched his head with vigorous impatience until I pulled up the article was nauseating. This was going so swimmingly.

"What is it?" he asked, as I handed him the phone. "Wait. I just read about this. Detective Smith was the one that arrested him."

"I think -" but before I could finish, someone interrupted me, and it was not someone that I wanted to be interrupted by.

"Miss Nova," Captain Sanders yelled out, storming down the hallway to approach me in the most dramatic manner. "Can I help you?" Wow, she clearly didn't want to see me. Maybe I shouldn't have accused her of ignoring rape victims, but in my opinion, that was debatable.

"Captain," I said, almost negatively acknowledging her presence. "Everything is fine. Detective Baron was just helping me out with some...logistical issues."

"Is that so?"

From what I could gather, Tom wasn't the Captain's favorite detective for whatever reason. Maybe he was on her last nerve, and he was working this case so she wouldn't have to. I wasn't sure, but I perceived her attitude as a little brash.

"Then I'm sure Detective Baron has already told you that we have no leads on the Rosa case."

"And I'm sure that you might know..." I stopped for a second not understanding why I started this sentence that way. Could I seriously have been any more awkward in this situation? "...Well, I might have something for you."

"Really?" She still hadn't dropped her condescending tone, but I didn't pay much attention. I was too busy trying to shove the article from my phone into her face. "What is this?"

"Brian Ruben. I think he was the one that hit my sister. Look at the date. His car had to go into the shop the day she was hit. They used to go out. Did you even bother to ask if they knew each other? They went to the same school. This town has like, what? Six thousand people? It doesn't take a genius to suspect that."

Captain Sanders kept her chin up with her eyes to the floor and bit her cheek the whole time, but not unconfidently. Like she was just waiting for me to shut up and knew the proper response to my accusations.

"Actually, Miss Rosa," she started. "Detective Baron here already questioned Brian Ruben last week."

Before I responded, they could see my eyes shoot wide open. Their theory of me just being a snotty, little teenager had now been confirmed true. At least in their eyes.

"What did you ask him? Are you sure it was about my sister?"

"Yes, Nova," Tom responded, finally speaking for himself. "I knew they were in a relationship, but I didn't know about the car accident he had. We really should take a look at that car, Captain."

"Hold it!" Captain Sanders yelled, even though we weren't going anywhere. "Detective, perhaps you should have read the full report on where Brian Ruben was the afternoon of the Rosa accident."

Was she serious? Did he really not read the entire file?

"Ma'am, what are you talking about?!" My patience for sounding like a proper, well-spoken adult officially ran out.

"The reason Mr. Ruben's car was in the shop was because he hit a police car."

Damn it. If this was true, I was back to square one.

"And you saw this happen?" I asked, just to be sure.

"No," she said, with a growing attitude. There was no way to redeem myself at this point. This woman thought I was an absolute idiot. "It happened on the other side of town right outside his home. There are pictures if you would like to see."

That couldn't have been true. Not about there being pictures, but there was no way they were going to let me see them. I guess she just wanted to continue to act stuck up.

"No. It's fine," I admitted through gritted teeth. I still refused to drop my teenager attitude. "I believe you, I guess. I just found it to be an insane coincidence, don't you think?" God that was painful to say.

Without even blinking, Captain Sanders looked me right in the eye and said, "I don't believe in coincidences."

"Neither do I," I said with the most confidence I'd had throughout the entire conversation. "And that's exactly my point."

A "goodbye", or "thank you" in this scenario was not necessary. At least in my opinion. So, I didn't give one. My rubber Doc Martens slammed on the ground especially hard as I stormed out of the station. And to be honest, I felt extremely self-conscious about the way I was walking. Or maybe I was just overthinking. I hate it when people think that I'm being unnecessarily stupid. Call me weird. Call me boring. Call me a loser. I really couldn't care less, but I don't like it when people think that I am being unreasonable. It does nothing but make me feel invalid. I'm not a pointless human being just wandering the earth.

Home was the last place I wanted to be at the moment. I knew my mother needed me pretty much all the time, but there were people that I needed too. Right then, I needed my sister. The woods didn't seem too far away. Once again, I ran like the wind.

I'm going to see my sister.

Thank God, or whoever it was that gave me this privilege, not that I believed in any of that crap, but whatever. I could do it now. I knew I could. No hesitation. No second guessing, or having my puny little hand lead me. I was gonna keep running to my sister until I was in her arms and not think about her being gone.

The bridge crept into my view. Right where I left it. As usual, I almost fell as I stumbled down the ditch and into the barren stream, but it didn't stall me in the slightest.

I could almost see the glimmer, the shine, and the radiance that was coming from under the bridge. Whatever it was, the source was powerful, and beyond beautiful. But it was the real kind of beauty. The beauty that you feel before you see.

I don't know which part of my body was the first to touch the entity, but after I closed my eyes, it was the longest three steps of my life, but I took them.

One, two, three, I subconsciously counted.

Everything felt slow with a little tingle rippling across my skin. I reopened my eyes to see the other world brighter than mine just like last time.

Something felt off, and I couldn't tell if it was a good off or not. But it made me run to my sister even faster. Lucky for me, I was already warmed up.

My house felt so far away. I reached for my phone when I was running, but what if my phone didn't work in this world?

Mindlessly I clicked on my sister's contact number anyways. Straight to voicemail. The last thing in the world that I wanted. The last time I tried to call her, I got sent straight to voicemail as well. That was because, unknown to me yet, she was already gone.

"Stop thinking about that," I told myself out loud. My feet switched back and forth even faster. My lungs didn't even notice the absence of oxygen or the heat in the air.

Finally, I reached my house. Unfortunately, I didn't know if she was there or not, but she was in this world. I could feel it. I could *see* it. Maybe it was just the glow and vibrancy surrounding me, but I swear to you, I could see it.

My feet still didn't stop as I stumbled up the stairs. I could hear laughter. Whose laughter it belonged to, I didn't know. But as I reached the top of the stairs, I could hear it coming from Veena's room.

Knock, knock, knock.

"Yeah?" I heard my sister say from behind the door.

"Can I come in?" I asked like a helpless little puppy.

"Yeah!"

The second before I opened the door, the pieces in my head snapped together like magnets, and I knew who was with her.

"What?" I heard Raya's snarly voice ask me. My arch enemy sat across Veena on her bed, staring at me with her snake eyes, and I hadn't even done anything yet.

"I'm here for my sister," I snapped back at her. What was she even doing here? Usually she would only hang out with my sister at our dad's house. My mom couldn't stand Raya. Of course, my mom never admitted it, but one could only hide Draco Malfoy forehead lines for so long. I overheard Raya complain about how my mom hated her all the time. Therefore, Raya hated being here.

"Can we...I don't know. Do something later?" I asked Veena while concentrating too hard on not making eye contact with Raya.

"Actually, I'm going out with Raya and the girls tonight. Is that okay? Can we do something another night?"

It was times like these I was reminded that I have absolutely no poker face.

"Why? Where are you two going?" My attitudinal hip popped so far out it could poke through an entire block of Gouda cheese. The sass.

44

"None of your business," said Raya. She then had the audacity to turn to my sister and laugh hysterically like a goddamn hyena. This was unfortunately for her, quite common, and I say *unfortunately for her* because my sister's common reaction was staring at her with the most blank, unimpressed face. Raya still never caught on. Idiot.

"Fine. I'll be in my room," I said as I slammed the door. Veena hated loud noises probably more than anything that I could think of, but she just ruined an important moment by not defending me. Who knew how long I would be able to come into this world? She was wasting my time.

Nonetheless, I laid on my bed with anger and rage shooting out of my head and toes. At least an hour went by until I put on some music and stopped lying there in silence like a serial killer. I was under the impression that Veena and Raya were gonna be done soon with whatever crap they were doing, but what did I know? I was just Veena's obnoxious little sister and literally nothing else.

About another two hours went by of me replaying Panic at the Disco songs and going in and out of an uncomfortable nap since I still hadn't taken my shoes off. Right before I was about to doze off for probably the fourth time, I heard a light knock that I could only hope was filled with regret and apologies.

"Hey," I heard Veena say. "Can I come in?"

I didn't bother to be dramatic and give her an unnecessary pause or an audible sigh before I answered. She would know I was just bullshitting her. So, I said, "Yeah," with the little energy that I had.

Veena ran in, hopped on the bed, and laid her body across the duvet as if nothing was wrong. Classic sister relationship.

"I talked to Raya," she stated.

"Abooooout?"

"About not being such an ass to you." I should have been shocked, but it was Veena. She always protected me in the end.

"It's about time," I said. "I barely survived sophomore year because of her."

"Well, what did you expect? You wouldn't leave us alone half the time!" If I was standing up, my jaw would have dropped straight to the floor, but instead my nose looked like it smelled spoiled milk.

"Really?" I was furious. "Are you serious right now? You have a million friends and I have a solid one! I wanna be around other people sometimes!"

Veena looked like she was about to have diarrhea. Then again, I should have felt lucky that I had a sister that *didn't* wanna tell me that she had no desire to have her little sister around all the time.

"Sometimes we want to hang out, just us friends, and it's different when you're younger." Veena kept scratching her back like she always did when she was uncomfortable.

"That's a pathetic excuse. We're like...what? Eighteen months apart?" I was honestly trying to do the math in my head, because for some strange reason I didn't know.

July...to February...wow. I really couldn't do math.

"I mean, maybe it'll be different when we're older. We'll technically be closer in age using a different perspective. I think most sisters get closer when they're older."

Such a touching, and true statement, and also the last thing that I wanted to hear. Hearing those words effortlessly flowing out of her mouth was like needles stabbing into my heart from all different directions. How could she not know the true reality? The reality where that storyline could never exist.

"I - I -" Words couldn't properly form with the stone scratching down my throat. Brushing it aside to see that my sister was right there in front of me didn't seem like an option, but it was. She was here. Maybe not in my world, but she was inches away from me. For just a second, I wanted a moment of peace, and I wanted to hug my sister without crying.

My arms grew a heart of their own and I threw my arms around her.

"Whoa," she exclaimed. "I thought you would still be mad at me, but I won't say no to this." I heard and felt a little giggle escape from her.

It only took me a few yet long moments for me to stop the tears from running. I let go to look at her face as if I was never gonna see it again.

"I'm sorry," I said to her with a puffy and red face. "I'm just tired...of a lot of things."

"You know that I'm always going to be with you, right? But you don't *always* need me."

46

Naturally, I cocked my head back with a touch of confusion. That was a weird and oddly insightful thing to say. Until then, I thought she didn't know anything about the other world. *My* world. But then, I was getting a sense that she didn't necessarily *know* anything, but she just knew she had to say that. Or maybe she just sensed it.

"Oh damn," I said to myself as I sat myself straight up.

"What?" Veena asked, looking at me like she always did when I was acting weird.

"Veena, I'm sorry, but I need to go." Before she said anything back to me I'd already popped up off my bed.

"Nova." I already didn't like where this was going. She usually called me "Nov". Nova was for when I stole her shirt or something of the sort. "It's almost dinner time. Where are you going?"

"If I told you, you wouldn't believe me." Well wasn't that just some great early 2000s, crappy Zac Efron line right there.

"Alright, just don't get caught." And for some reason she laid back down on *my* bed. *Dude, you have your own.*

I started to run out my bedroom door, but I forgot something. "I love you," I said as I whipped my hair back around to look at her. I just stared at her instead of casually saying it as I left, which may have seemed weird, but I really needed her to say it back.

"I love you too, Nov." There it was.

This time, I walked back to the bridge. I needed a break from running and I desperately needed to think. I'd been so focused on how this world could possibly exist and how I could pass between this world and mine that I hadn't thought about why it was there in the first place. The bridge portal didn't work for Jack, so why did it work for me? Did it *only* work for me? This was the one thing I couldn't get off my mind; could there be more than one reason why it was there?

Once again, I reached the bridge. This time the only reason I didn't hesitate to cross was because I could feel the urgency for something on the other side. Someone needed me. Actually, many people needed me, but the most important person was my sister. I was the one that needed closure, but she deserved to know who had hit her and then left her for someone else to bring to the hospital, only to die in the ambulance.

I could feel the determination as I passed under the bridge. The next step that I had to take was still unclear to me, but I knew I could figure it out soon and fast. But as soon as I stepped foot on the other side of the bridge, the determination vanished and all that was left was emptiness. Emptiness that was painful, and tugged at every nerve and cell in my body. It felt like my organs were somehow rearranging to become a different species of mammal. Only a few people experienced this. Somehow, I knew that to be true.

My knees instantly became weaker, and I had no desire to lift my head to meet eye level. All of the energy from my body steamed off my soul. The muscles in my legs knew no reason to support the rest of my body, and my knees impaled the soil below me. There was no question as to why this was happening. Veena. She felt so far away. The initial pain of her passing rushed back into me all over again.

A few minutes before, I physically acknowledged the confidence rising in me. A plan was developing. Then, it was almost as if someone performed conscious surgery, but they forgot to put all of my organs back in. Thank God I was still human at least. This couldn't last for long. I wouldn't allow it. There was a plan that I had to put in place.

My bum and upper body tucked-and-rolled over onto my back as my hair absorbed the dirt on the ground like a sponge. Just for a moment, I needed to breathe a normal breath. A breath that I hadn't taken in what felt like a lifetime.

My eyes slowly reopened, and all I could see was a cylindrical view of the trees surrounding me with the sky scattered on top. This was my world that still contained so much beauty, but it wasn't the world that I wanted to be in, and I was never going to.

One time I heard that if you breathe through your nose for long enough, it reduces anxiety. Well, I was gonna need more than reduced anxiety, but I tried it anyway. I just needed the strength to stand back up. I owed my sister that much.

When I finally stood back up, it was one of those times where I was barely even thinking about it, and instead my AHwhatever just led me there. I didn't acknowledge the misery of hoisting myself into the air much. I was up and mobile. Slowly, but still moving, and it was time to get to work.

My feet didn't pick up a ton of speed as I worked my way out of the woods, and my eyes refused to tear away from the dirt, rocks, and leaves. It was time to sing a song in my head. Don't ask me why. It was just one of those times.

"Here comes the sun, do, do, do, do."

Man, I'm an old woman. And MAN, that's a good song. Those freaking Beatles slayed. I wouldn't say that it was my favorite song, and it wasn't Veena's either, but it was kind of like our song. For some reason I couldn't remember why, but we always used to randomly sing it together.

"Little Darlin', it's been a long cold -"

"Nova?"

All at the same time, my feet stopped in their tracks, my shoulders tensed up like they always did, and my eyes widened. I knew that voice, but I was afraid to look. Even more afraid than when I heard my sister's voice after she died. Somehow, I gathered up enough energy and courage to lift my gaze and see Raya walking towards me with her flashiest yellow skirt.

"Nova." So now she decided to call me by my real name and not some crude nickname like emo monkey? "How are you?" Still not a hello, but I'll take it.

"Um...hey...uhh." How in the hell was I supposed to answer *her*? "I'm sorry. You took me by surprise. I wasn't expecting to see you or anyone here. It's kind of my lonesome walking place."

It was only a half a second long, but I swear she popped the corners of her mouth into a brief smile.

"Sorry to bother you. I was actually just walking to my house."

"You live around here?" Welp, didn't know that fun fact.

"Yeah. Just a few streets over." I could sense the awkward silence coming on, but in just a tiny heartbeat, she proved me wrong. "Look, Nova." Oh, boy please give me the awkward silence instead of this. "I really miss your sister. She should have dumped me as a friend so long ago, and mainly for how I treated you."

I didn't mean to, but my interruption just slipped out. "Yeah, it's fine. I was really annoying. Still am."

"Yeah I know," she laughed. "But who cares? That's no excuse. And I'll never be able to forgive myself for how pathetic I am for not realizing that until now. It shouldn't have taken...what happened for me to notice that."

The pause. She wasn't able to say it yet. The pain. She was hurting, and she was hurting deep. Made sense. They were always together.

"I just feel lost without her," she continued with a few more tears running down her face. "And I just haven't been able to stop thinking about how much worse it must be for you." She clearly saw the shift in my face. It wasn't a negative reaction, but she probably took it as one. "I'm sorry. I'm not trying to shove my emotions in your face, but I just never want anybody to feel the way I'm feeling ever again, and it sucks that I don't have any control over that, and you know how much of a control freak I am."

The emptiness in her eyes. It was the same emptiness that my family and I had in our eyes for what felt like way too long now. I didn't know if Raya was pulling my leg right here, but it didn't matter. At least not in this moment.

Raya looked down, started scratching her wrists and said, "I don't have many other friends. At least not friends like Veena, but she was always so kind to my little sister. No shocker there, but if it were me instead of Veena, I would want someone looking out for my little sister, Rori. Wherever I would be, I would be really worried   about   her."

I was about to say that I really didn't need anyone to look after me, but once again, she got to it first. "I know you're tough and all that. I just - I won't be able to sleep at night knowing you're in more pain than I am. And I'm so sorry I didn't say anything to you at the funeral. I honestly just didn't want to bother you, and I wasn't sure what to say to you yet. And I don't expect you to forgive me, but I just really wanted to tell you all of that."

Then came the awkward silence. Or at least it was only awkward because I didn't know what to say. Day by day even after her death, my sister was still making a difference in people's lives. And let's be real, I really wanted Raya to think I was cool when I was younger. What's eight years too late, really?

For now, I knew what she needed, because it was what I needed too, and I hope she never found out what it was like to lose a sister, even though she kind of already did. Nonetheless, I gave her a genuine, warm, almost teary-eyed smile and slowly came into a gentle hug, and to my surprise, she hugged me back.

PART 5: JULY, 23RD, 5:27PM

Later that day, my dad called and told me he wanted me to stay over at his house that night. No problem with that or anything, but I could almost guarantee my mom had to encourage him to ask me. John was a shy guy that had a horrible time showing his emotions to other people. Expressing emotion to himself? That was a different thing entirely. I heard him crying like a baby when Robin Williams died, I could only imagine how much he cried alone when he got the call about my sister.

Anyway, when I went over, we had dinner, popcorn, root beer floats, and watched *Jeopardy*. Most of this quality time together included minimal talking. Which again, fine, but I really needed to figure out how to get my dad to open up to other people, especially me. Veena was usually the one he would tell his dating gossip to and things like that, but only sometimes when my sister could carefully slink her way into his brain. He'd always been one of those parents who thought that they needed to be strong in front of their children and vulnerability was a weakness. Veena would know what to do.

The only hassle was that I had plans to visit the crash site, and Veena's route to work was surprisingly further away from my dad's house than I thought. It would have been easier if I was at my mom's, but it wasn't like I could tell my dad what I was planning to do. Man, these early morning sneak outs were getting tiresome, and I was not excited for the day that I got caught. But then again, my dad worked really late nights at the garage. So he was gonna be dead asleep until three in the afternoon at the earliest.

Just in case somebody saw me and recognized me en route, I wore my black hoodie with a black beanie and kept my head down most of the way. Adults are such snitches. Unfortunately, wearing a black hoodie in the middle of July was a poor decision, and it took me even longer to get to the crash site. Genius.

Finally, after about an hour, I got to the scene of the crime. Although the second that I got there, my eyes automatically drifted in the opposite direction. It was like watching people kiss when you're the only person in the room. Looking was just not an option, but no matter what, it was still beyond uncomfortable.

"Duuuude," I whispered to myself. "Come on, you can do this. You gotta look. You didn't run for an hour to wuss out."

Most people would take a deep breath in, close their eyes, reopen them, and slowly turn around. But of course, that's for normal people, and I didn't think being able to cross over into a different universe classified as "normal". So, what did I do? I bent my knees into a mini squat, jumped up into the air, and turned around. Why? Because what you see in the movies is absolute bullshit, and it's always better to rip the Band-Aid off. I said what I said.

There was nothing ultimately disturbing at the scene that still remained. It was just the stabbing memory that I had to push through. When I get my driver's license, I will take the long route if it meant avoiding driving through this place. No way.

Now, don't get me wrong, I knew the likelihood of me finding anything was extremely low, but I had to know. Things like this didn't happen often in our tiny little town. The chances of the police missing something, was probably high, considering the lack of experience.

I could see the skid marks from the tires. It was obvious which pair belonged to which car. One of them went fairly straight and then suddenly crooked and off the road, and the other met with the ongoing tire's sudden slant and then went around in one giant circle. Everything about the scene screamed violence. I almost had to look away. *Oh God, what did they do to her?*

"Stop," I had to physically and harshly say to myself. Now was not the time for emotions. They would get in the way. Blind me. But before I could wipe any emotion from my body, I had to acknowledge this piercing thought and give myself just a touch of hope, and I deeply hoped she didn't suffer.

Okay, back to work. What was I even looking for? What would the hyper-fictionalized detectives on the unrealistic T.V. shows do? They would probably say she was part of a drug institution or something and say this was a masterful plot of revenge. But damn those shows were good. Too bad I wouldn't be able to watch any episodes about hit and runs anymore.

Maybe they would have some good recommendations. What would they actually do to initiate their first steps? My eyes locked with the trails of tire rubber when it finally hit me like a pathetic fish whacking its tiny little tail in my face, reminding me how dumb I was. Of course, they would simply follow the path of the predator.

"Follow the tires," I said way too proudly. The more I thought about it, the more I realized a nine-year-old who watches *Paw Patrol* could figure that out.

My feet touched the beginning of the skid marks from the suspect's car. If only I knew a single damn thing about cars, maybe I would be able to tell what kind of car it was, but on the other hand I lived an interesting life and straight up didn't care.

Anyways, my eyes followed the tire tracks inch by inch, but I didn't notice anything unusual. That was, until my AHwhatever stopped getting in the way of being a normal human being. *Geez.* Why didn't this hit me right away? Why were there skid marks on the road before the collision? It's like the suspect zoomed off all of a sudden.

We already ruled out the suspect doing this on purpose, and I was happy to admit; that did make sense. Why would they collide going in opposite directions? Wouldn't it be easier to follow her and then run her off the road? Fishy.

In my notes application, I wrote down anything that I noticed, and I took as many pictures as I could in every angle, even if I didn't see anything. Although, as I reached the end of the suspect's skid marks, there was something that was rather conspicuous.

"Is that a footprint?" I asked myself. It wasn't. It was half a footprint. The ball of the foot, to be more specific. As if they were running.

Dude. Bingo. I was right, or I guess the police were right too. If this person was running out of their car, it was an accident. Who would frantically run out of their car after doing something on purpose? The cars didn't light on fire or anything. And if they did it on purpose, they would have just kept driving.

Damn, I was good.

What else? I could barely see any other foot prints on the passenger's side of the car. That was the only one. Wait. The passenger's side? From how the skid marks ended, it looked like they hit Veena's car head on. Why would the driver need to come out of the passenger's side? The driver's door shouldn't have been damaged. Unless there was more than one person in the car. I needed to get a look at that police report. There was no way that information was in there. Technically I had no evidence to back that theory up, but I just knew.

"What else? What else? What else?" I muttered to myself as I took more and more pictures of what was probably nothing.

A few glass shards scattered across the side of the road. My lack of knowledge in cars didn't hamper me in knowing how tinted my sister's car windows were. So I could tell most of the glass was from her car. Even after a few seconds of taking more pictures, I had to take a break from looking. That weird feeling. It came back again, and there was nothing I could do. AHwhatever wasn't going to help me here. All I could feel was her pain, even though I hoped I would never fully understand what she felt.

That was enough pictures. I got all I needed, or at least I thought I did. For some reason, I figured it would be easier if I just scrolled through the past few snaps of the glass to see if I would notice anything.

Nothing out of the ordinary, but something did catch my eye. My fingers went on autopilot as I scrolled through the pictures of the glass, and as I came to the last one something was off in the bottom left hand corner that I didn't see before.

"Is that...?"

The glass looked almost blue. It wasn't from Veena's car. Also, if it was from a headlight, Veena didn't have that kind of color on her headlights. It had to be from the suspect's car.

"Shit. Where is it? Where is it?" I used references from the picture to find out where it was, but shit, it took me a long time. Finally, after carefully searching through the dirt like I was both following and trying not to step on a family of ants, I found it. And damn straight, I was right.

Carefully, I used my sleeve to pick the glass and gently blow off all of the dirt. From the shape and texture, I could now tell for certain it was from the headlight of a car. If only I could know for certain if it was from the suspect's car. Who knew how long this had been there? On the other hand, how many other car accidents had happened in this exact spot? Not even a single car had passed by since I got there.

Vrooooooom.

Welp, spoke too soon.

Hiding seemed unnecessary, so I just walked along the street casually with a piece of glass in my pocket. From my point of view, everything about my appearance seemed normal and casual. Nothing conspicuous. Then again, I wasn't the police.

All of a sudden, all I could hear was the obnoxious, murderous sound of a siren. Although when I turned around to check it out, it wasn't a cruiser, it was a black Chevy with red and blue beaming out of the windows like a One Direction concert. It was a detective, and as the car creeped closer and closer to me I could see the face of the detective that I still couldn't remember the name of through the window. Crap, I'm a terrible person.

"Miss Rosa?" The detective asked.

"It's Nova, please. That's weird...Tom!" There we go.

"What are you doing here?"

"I might ask you the same thing." Truly, I didn't mean to ask that question or be so weird about it, but the more I thought about it, I did have a point.

It took him a few seconds to finally say, "Just a few follow up things."

No. That didn't seem right, but was that a good thing? Was he lacking faith in his colleagues?

"Really?" I asked with the most sass I could produce. He needed to start talking.

"In a way. I guess."

"Was the flashing really necessary?"

"I just wanted to see if it was you. Forgive me, I'm not too familiar with the back of your head. Just wanted to make sure." No cracking yet, but I was coming close. "So, you didn't answer my question."

No point in hesitation or lying. "Wanted to see some things for myself. The captain isn't giving me a lot of reassurance."

"I don't blame you." It's not that I was shocked that he thought this, but I was surprised that he admitted it to me. "What did you find?"

Would it be unbalanced to tell him my theories? If anything, he was probably just gonna tell me that it was insufficient evidence and no jury would convict with what I had. But what would I have to lose? He might have to take the evidence with him, but it's not like it was gonna disappear. With that, my shoulders twitched while crunching to my ears, and I pulled the crucial piece of evidence out of my pocket and held it in front of my eye like a grape.

"This might seem stupid," I began to defend myself, "but this piece of glass was in the pile of glass along with my sister's but it's not from my sister's car. Now how many -"

"Yeah, I see what you're saying." Wow. Apparently, this dude had a lot of surprises and tricks up his sleeves.

"I know you have to take it -"

"No," he interrupted me again. What was he talking about? It was *evidence*. I didn't know how to do this forensics crap, but withholding evidence was...what? A felony or something?

"What do you mean?" I asked after realizing I hadn't said anything yet.

"Do you drink coffee? Or hot chocolate or something?" Why was he changing the subject, but more importantly....

"How old do you think I am?" Truly, I love hot chocolate, but I was trying to be taken seriously here. "Coffee."

Tom got us iced coffees at this hidden gem that was extremely unadvertised and deserved more credit. Nobody else was there, but we still hid in the corner to prevent eavesdroppers from being nosy.

A few days earlier when I first saw the mess that was Tom - whatever his last name was - he seemed frantic and unorganized. Now, he looked stern, focused, and serious. I preferred the other Tom. Or at least I thought I did.

"So, is there anything about your sister's case that we should know about? Something that you haven't told us?"

That wasn't how I was expecting the conversation to start. Somehow, it kinda sounded like I was the new suspect, but then I realized that the answer was, indeed, "yes", and I was just being paranoid.

Everything that I knew, I told him. It wasn't much more, but he now knew my theory about the footprint, and Veena's diary. The diary probably wasn't relevant, but just in case. He needed to know *everything*. For most of the conversation, Tom sat there with his eyes to the table and his intertwined fists under his nose.

"Alright." That was the only thing he said for way too long, while I twiddled my thumbs and thought of other places that I rather would have been. "I think you have some things here that are worth looking into."

Finally cracked him.

"I knew you'd break eventually," I said, taking a big, dramatic gulp of my coffee.

"You did?"

"No. I'm just being a pain in the ass." Clearly, he hadn't warmed up to my bad humor yet, and from his face I could read that he was used to people making fun of him. "Can I ask you something?"

"Of course."

"Why are you being so secretive and weird about asking me these things? Couldn't you just call me on the phone or bring me into the station again?"

This was the question that he was dreading to answer. The stress in his temples was unnerving, but what if his actions could benefit me?

"Because I don't trust that...from what I've seen...I have suspicions. I'm not entirely sure what that means yet, but I think it means the station might be hiding something."

Surprise? It shouldn't have been, but this was something I didn't really consider. I just thought they sucked at their jobs, but could they be straight up lying? And even more intriguing, was this whole lying business Captain Sanders' idea?

"What do you mean? Like they could be covering for someone?" If I made my voice any softer it would have been considered an ASMR video.

"Honestly, I think it was someone's kid or something that could have hit her and they don't want to come forward."

Suddenly, it all made sense. That's why they were trying to blame it all on my sister. But who were they trying to cover up for?

"What makes you think all this?"

Before he answered he pulled out a file folder labeled, "CONFIDENTIAL" on the front with my sister's name on the tab. But instead of opening it up, he slapped it down on the table right in front of me.

"Open it up. See if you notice anything."

The thought of opening up a confidential police file made my head hurt and my knuckles ache. Doing it in front of a detective only made it worse. Ironic.

With shaky hands, I slowly opened up the file. Now, I wasn't any law enforcement official, but I was pretty sure there should have been more information and like...I don't know...papers than what was in this thing. Although, as I continued to flip through the few forms that were in the folder, I took an educated guess that there probably was more information in this thing at one point.

"Why does this singular paper have a staple in it?" I asked Tom.

"I was wondering the same thing. For some reason, Sanders barely wants me to touch the case even though it's not closed yet."

Anger began to initiate in my throat and then spread to my neck. Veena deserved better than this. How would I be able to look her in the eye without pouring out the disaster that was the truth?

"Legally, what can we do about this?" I asked him with a quivering chin and flaming eyes, but at that moment, I assumed there *was* nothing to do. Going up against the police? Especially when their strongest instinct was probably to protect their child at all cost? We'd be lucky if we could get them to tell us where the bathroom was at the station. What could I say? Cops are assholes.

"I was hoping you would have an idea." This guy knew I wasn't even old enough to drive, right?

"Why are you asking me? Did nobody else listen to you at the station?"

"I didn't tell anybody about this at the station." Okay, maybe that was a dumb question because obviously he hadn't. But that only furthered my point in why the hell I was being consulted on confidential police business. "Everything that you said to Sanders...I guess I understood where you were coming from."

Before I could even fully process what he said, my back slammed up against the back of the chair and my arms crossed on autopilot like a doctor's knee jerk reflex test. The tightness in his eyes and jaw leaked immediate regret.

"That didn't come out right." He shook with hyper-anxiety. "I mean, that's not what I meant." Damn straight, dude. "What I mean is; you were right. But something else isn't right."

Alright, fine. He got it. I went back to listening, and curiosity overwhelmed me once more.

"Continue," my assertive voice commanded.

"First, keep in mind I've only been a detective for a short period of time." Every nerve in my body wanted to respond to that little reminder with *Reallyyyy?* Thank God I successfully resisted. "And Sanders has only been Captain for less than a year now, but something is off. She doesn't usually keep secrets. She says what's on her mind. Exactly what's on her mind in case you haven't noticed."

Well if that wasn't the truth.

"Are you implying that Sanders is trying to cover up for her kid?"

"No. Sanders doesn't have any children. What I'm saying is that somebody is probably trying to cover up for somebody that they care about, if not a child, and I think Sanders knows about it. I think Sanders knows who's hiding something."

Everything in me wanted to shove all of the fractured thoughts from my head into the bottomless pit that is my stomach. At least I would poop it out eventually. This was going to change my life forever. I thought my life had already altered as much as it ever possibly could when my sister died. But then I found a supernatural portal that led me to my deceased sister, and I stood corrected. Now, I am finding out that government corruption could be the fatal destruction of Veena's investigation. Once again, I stood corrected.

"Okay. I say we back this up," I said, somehow managing to produce some sense.

"How so?"

"The other people investigating this case, what did they find out, or discover that wasn't in this file? Any talk going around? Or - I dunno." Maybe I shouldn't have had such a stick up my ass when I told the police how to do their jobs because that sentence probably made zero sense.

"I can't think anything off the top of my head, but I'm sure I could -" His lips pursed as if he was raging with sass and a hint of anger, but I guess he just had a peculiar thinking face.

"What is it?" I asked with less patience than a teething puppy.

"You know that gas station down the street from where...the accident happened?"

He could not have made that more cringey to hear, but I appreciated his attempt at censorship.

"Yeah, I've seen it a few times."

"We don't know the exact time of the crash, but we have a frame. Dodge's Gas Station has security cameras in their parking lot. If we can get a hold of them, we can see which cars passed on the road during that hour. There can't be too many."

Finally. Some real detective work beamed from this guy. Suddenly, some confidence spiraled up my gut and into the back of my head. I could trust Tom, but there were still some things that I obviously had to keep from him. The question was; would he be able to read that from me, and lose trust in me? He was my only hope of getting justice for my sister. Carelessness had no value here.

"Let's go to the gas station tomorrow," I commanded. "Or can I come with you? Would we get caught or - ?" And just like that, the very last person that I expected to see in this hidden coffee shop walked straight through the door and stomped right up to me; freaking Charlotte Rosa. Damn it, I was so ready to go to a college far faaaar away from here.

"Mom? What the hell are you doing here?"

"Oh, surely you can swear better than that, honey." Damn, Charlotte. The sass. Unusual for her, but in an odd way refreshing. "I saw you in the window with Detective Baron, and I'm just really curious as to why."

She popped one hip out to the side and slammed her hand on it like she was digging a hole. I take back that refreshing part.

"He was asking me more stuff about Veena, obviously." She had to believe that, right?

60

"Really? Any reason as to why you're doing it in a coffee shop?" Crap. Sometimes I forgot where Veena got her smarts from.

"Mom, we were just -"

"Detective, I really don't find it appropriate for you to be in a coffee shop, alone with a fifteen-year-old girl. Especially when you look very young for your age. People will think less of you."

Ouch. Charlotte was not holding back.

"Sh - Oh, Mrs. Rosa. I'm sorry, I didn't mean to - I mean - I really did just need to ask her a few questions."

She wasn't buying *anything*. Even though it was...ya know...the truth. I could tell I was done for when she didn't respond to anything that Tom said and just pulled me up by my arm and dragged me out of the coffee shop. On top of that, she didn't even let me bring the rest of my coffee with me. Rude.

"Mom, come on. You're overreacting."

"Oh, really? I don't think pulling you out of meddling in a serious police investigation is overreacting. Believe it or not, I'm trying to protect you. Doing things like this could be considered a felony. I don't need both of my kids taken away from me."

Now was the time to stop talking...about everything. Sometimes I really hated how well she could read me. It was never useful, but I could read her pretty well too. Besides, she did have a point. I needed to keep her mind at ease, and just be more careful while investigating anything that I could.

"And by the way, you're grounded for a month."

PART 6: JULY 25TH, 10:30PM

For the past fifteen years that I'd been alive, my mother had grounded me for the dumbest reasons that any human being on this earth could think of. One time I was grounded for logging onto her computer to see what my homework was on the school website. Funny thing was, I asked her if I could, and she said yes. She was just too distracted by the T.V. that she didn't notice it was me and not my sister. Now whose fault was that, really? What kind of mother couldn't tell her own children apart?

This time was a little different. Obviously, I knew that I shouldn't have been messing with police business, but what business were they really doing? Also, I always guessed that my mom was the type of mother that would do anything for her children. I guess, in a way, she is because she thought that she was protecting me, but wouldn't she be doing this herself if she could? Charlotte Rosa's damn smart. A hell of a lot smarter than me, but she had the confidence of a walrus. That probably didn't make any sense, but walruses are weird.

Alright. What was there that I could do from my room? Tom was still on my side, and I trusted him to do the right thing, believe me, but I still wasn't confident that he wasn't gonna screw things up. That gave me horrible guilt thinking that. Especially because I could relate to him so much. Everyone thought that I was a screw up too.

At this point, the only person that I knew that had never screwed anything up in their entire life was Jack. That kid would be the biggest teacher's pet if he wasn't so goddamn awkward and the teachers weren't so homophobic like the oldies they were.

That afternoon, I filled Jack in on everything over the phone. Well...not everything. But I told him about what Tom discovered and about being hella grounded. After I was done ranting, it got me thinking. What would I be able to reveal to him without him knocking me out and saying "I was just trying to knock some sense into you."? (Trust me, he would at least do something like that.) It's not like I had any proof. He couldn't go through the portal. It was just for me. If I brought something back from the other world either; one, it would disappear when I crossed back over, or two, Jack would just say something like, "You just brought that over from your house," and that would make sense because the two worlds were pretty damn similar. I was in desperate need of a solid plan.

"Can you come over and climb up to my window?" I texted Jack. He'd only ever done that once, and, yes, I was grounded then too. Jack never needed to sneak up to my room. My mom knew how gay he was. She didn't care, unless I was grounded. Obviously.

"Do I have to?" Jack texted back. Blatantly, he was just being a whiny little baby because he was the least athletic person in our school, but the last time he did it, he was able to pull himself back up when his feet slid off one of the vines. So I really didn't know what he was complaining about.

"Come on. I need your help with something, and I told you I was grounded."

"I can't assist from over the phone?"

"Trust me, you're going to want to be fully present for this one."

It took him way too long to get to my house. The clock was about to strike midnight. His parents always went to bed by nine because they had him in their forties, and my mom had the T.V. on so loud, she would die if she fell asleep during a fire. Nothing to worry about, except for Jack breaking his neck. I wondered if a pulley system was worth investing in.

"Yo!" Jack hollered from down below. That was probably the second or third time he ever said *yo* in his life.

"Would you be quiet?" I loudly whispered out my window. "Come on!"

In the least creepy way possible, I watched the top of his head slowly progress toward me. Very, very, slowly.

Finally, when Jack reached the top and I pulled him into my room, he popped right up with one of the proudest looks I'd ever seen on his face.

"You didn't fall?" I said, shocked, almost immediately regretting it.

"I didn't! Those push-ups are paying off!"

"You've been going to the gym?"

Jack almost keeled over with laughter before he responded, "No. Just push-ups."

"Modified?"

"Obviously." Regardless of his almost impressive accomplishment, he still collapsed onto my bed and continued to audibly gasp for air. "So, what do you need me for that's just so important?"

"God, where do I even begin?" Anxiety started to tickle up my spine and creep into my fingertips. There were a few ways I could go about this. Okay, maybe there were just two. One, I could spit it out, or two, I could ease it into him with no striking punch line. "I might need your help with a few things." Good place to start.

"Yeah, I know. You always do." Not wrong.

"I know, I know. It's just, I might need an extra hand in the investigation."

Before Jack snapped up off my bed, he rolled over to give me the most asshole, perplexed look I'd ever received from anyone.

"You're still getting involved? Are you kidding? You're going to get caught again. Your mom is like a hawk that can transform into a snake and slither around in places you can't see with a naked eye." Geez. That went into detail. "And besides, Nova, I don't think running around with this detective guy is such a good idea. What if he's a total creep?"

"Dude, how dumb do you think I am? I know better than that. If he makes me feel weird, then I'll just leave it's fine. Trust me."

Reasoning with Jack wasn't my strong suit, but the shift in his weight told me he believed me and trusted me.

"Alright, fine. What do you need me to do?"

He wasn't gonna like this shit. "I need you to distract Charlotte, and I need you to tell her that we've got like a school project that we have to work on or something."

"Love, it's summer. Are you feeling okay?" Like my mother he put the back of his sweaty and dirty hand to my forehead, but with reason.

"I'm like ninety-five percent sure that I'm feeling fine, but I need to go somewhere and soon...and for a while."

"Where?"

To see Veena, dumbass. But how was I gonna explain that? Still, he was getting closer.

"You don't wanna know." Biting my lip usually came in handy when I was nervous about saying something crazy, which was surprisingly more often than the average human. "But I will tell you if you really want me to."

Jack pushed back his curly, Heath Ledger locks over his ears indicating that he was listening with the sass he was born to embrace.

"Okay." I pulled him down on the bed and refused to let go of his scrawny, little wrist as I began my life altering news. "I've never believed in psychics and stuff like that. You know that, right?"

Jack's facial expressions were on fire tonight. Especially when he asked me, "Where in the hell is this going?"

"Be patient!...You - you know how sometimes after a giant and dramatic loss, people will see their loved ones for just a brief moment? Or at least they think they do?"

As his eyes softened with sympathy, Jack clasped right back onto my arm and said, "Oh. Shit. I heard about this a lot, yeah. I was afraid this was going to happen to you. Honestly, I thought it would happen to your mom before you, but -"

"Right, right, but here's the catch; I have to go to a certain place to see her. It's a little more supernatural than most people are used to or comfortable with...." Wow, that was the wrong method to use. I'm the Band-Aid girl, why did I think this was gonna work?

65

I didn't even have the guts to look up at Jack's face. I knew it would just be either Chad's face on *Saturday Night Live* or Cher's face from *Clueless,* but probably a mixture of both.

"Seriously, I can get you some Tums or Ibuprofen."

"Stop. Stop. I really need you to believe me. Listen. There's this special place in the woods that has some sort of spiritual gift. Veena is there, and it's like she never left."

Jack probably didn't even realize he was doing it, but his upper body slowly leaned away from me inch by inch, but his eyes told me a completely different story. It was as if the idea of spirituality dawned on him for the very first time. I'm convinced this was the face he made when he was beyond sure of his sexuality.

"You should have seen the look on my face when I saw her. It was like a fairytale, a dark fairytale at first, but it was also like she never left. That is, after I got over the shock. This place...it's like it's another dimension or something. But it's there for me, to help me." Telling him this was like telling him I won the lottery. Joy and celebration were called for, but no matter how exciting it was, you know you're going to resent paying half of what you just won in taxes and you couldn't get that thought out of your head. But regardless, I couldn't stop smiling.

"That's...interesting." His voice quivered with the most tasteful mix of confusion and fear.

"I know. Take your time."

"Nova," he finally leaned back toward me and took my hand once more. "It's not that I don't believe you, but I think your mind might be taking it a little too far somehow."

"What's that supposed to mean?" I snapped, genuinely confused, but I was still somewhat impressed with the fact that he at least somewhat believed me.

"Have you gone to visit her grave yet?"

Grave. The moment that word peeled off his lips, I had a new word that I despised and dreaded. The answer to his question was *no*, but for some reason I felt incredibly guilty admitting it, so instead I just answered by letting my focus fall to the floor.

"I think it would be healthy," Jack continued. "Maybe you would stop seeing her."

"Right, but it's a little more complicated than that. I know that I should visit her, but I don't think I'll be able to stop seeing her until I figure out who did this to her. That's why she's here in this other world, so I can say a proper goodbye and so she can help me solve the case."

Jack struggled to find the right words. They got lost in his throat. A few of them almost came out, but it was like I was speaking gibberish to him.

"Okay, here's the deal," he finally said. "I will do whatever you need me to do, but you need to promise me two things."

"Depends on what those two things are." Of course I would agree to whatever they were, but I needed to make myself seem more sane and assertive.

"I need you to promise me you will go and visit Veena's grave and I need you to go and talk to someone. I promise you that I will go with you to both. Only if you want me to. You know I will. I don't want to tell you what you're seeing, but I think whatever is going on in your head will go back to normal if you promise to do those two things."

Thank God I had him in my life. Honestly, I could tell Jack that I was off to commit cold-blooded murder and he would probably say to me, "Okay, but first take a jacket; it's cold out." He always had my back.

"I can do all of that."

"That's my girl. Now is there anything else I can do?"

Before I told him, I cracked a little smile. His attitude was about to completely change. "I need you to hide under my covers and pretend to be me if my mom or Ralph comes in."

"What?" Told you. "Why?"

"I can't get caught again, and I really need to be helping with this case. I told you, something weird is going on at the station. They're covering for someone's kid, or maybe even a politician."

"Why would they be covering up for a politician?"

"Have you been paying attention to politics in this country lately?"

"Unfortunately."

I couldn't think of anyone who they could be covering up for, but that was my whole point. I needed more information. As much as I could get. Someone needed to go behind bars.

"Pleeaaaase?" The puppy face NEVER worked on this boy, but at this point it was my only hope. "We can sleep until I need to leave and you can keep sleeping until someone comes in."

"Fine." Well, I'll be damned. It worked.

"Thank you, thank you, thank you! I promise you I will be safe, and it will all be worth it." Something was missing. Maybe it wasn't completely appropriate, but I felt the need for our handshake. So, what did I do as Jack stared me down? I held out my hand in hopes he would reciprocate. But before I needed to pull out my puppy face again, he disapprovingly shook his head, and with two pats on the palm, a slide down each other's forearms, and the least sassy snaps in the history of finger snaps, we completed our handshake.

A few hours later I crawled out of my window like the ninja I'd become. I could probably do it blind folded by now. Years ago, I named the vine Jeffrey when it first started to grow. Jeffrey held up pretty well.

Once again, like always, my ankles tingled as I stabbed my feet into the hard soil. I did my usual little shake, told myself to stop jumping so far down, and began to run until I realized that I just ate goldfish for breakfast and a terrible runner's cramp screwed itself into my stomach. Walking it was.

A few minutes into my slow, slow walk, my phone buzzed in my pocket. A call from a random number popped up, but my instincts shouted at me that it had to be Tom.

"Nova," said the voice of Detective Baron. Look who was right. "Are you on your way? You know I can still go alone. You don't have to come. The sun is barely up."

"Hey, Detective," I said, trying not to sound pathetically out of breath. "No, I should be there. You might need a hand. I'm five minutes away." I said good-bye and tucked my phone back in my pocket and gathered up enough energy to speed walk.

When I finally reached the gas station, I oddly enough felt an urge to hide, or at least subtly approach whoever was in there. This evidence was crucial, it could be a breaking point. I knew myself well enough to know that even if I stumble or hiccup on my presentation in the slightest bit, everything could take a turn for the worst. I had to be careful.

"Nova!" Tom called out from behind me, a few yards away from the door. "You ready?"

"No, but let's go anyway." I thought I heard nervous laughter coming from him, but I didn't wanna be any more annoying than I already was.

The interior part of the gas station was a complete surprise. I'd always taken pride in my robust sense of smell, and the second I stepped through the double doors, a waft of citrus breeze shot up my nose. It forced me to shut my eyes and take in the pleasant fragrance, but when I reopened them, all I saw was color coordinated items stacked on the shelves, polished and perfectly painted floors, and high-tech checkout gear. Who was running this place and how did they keep it up? All I knew was that if this was how organized they were in their store, they definitely kept solid records of their security.

"Hello," said Tom to the clerk behind the counter.

"How can I help you?"

Oh no. I didn't know the kid. I had never seen him before, but he had the most beautiful brown eyes and gorgeous Italian skin. It didn't happen that often to me, but sometimes I got too jittery to talk to attractive boys my age. Or at least too jittery to make any sense.

"We have some questions about the hit and run that happened down the street from here about two weeks ago," Tom seemed pretty official. I decided to let him do all the talking.

"Well, I didn't have anything to do with it. I wasn't working that day, but I did hear about it. Sounds horrible."

"That would be correct. It was. Nobody has come forward yet, and we understand you might have some security footage of the street. Which means you could have some crucial evidence as to which car could possibly have hit the poor girl. Could we take a look?"

"Oh, no way. Sorry."

Was he serious? Now I wasn't afraid to talk.

"Why is that?" I asked Mr. Pretty Boy. He was going to need to do some serious explanation.

"My dad's the boss here. He ain't gonna just let you see it without a paper or whatever it's called." A *warrant*, mansplainer person. A warrant. If only I had the guts to actually say that to him.

"Excuse me, young man, this could be crucial evidence in a serious case." Jesus, Tom. You already said that.

"Bro, I'll get in so much trouble. He's really strict about, well like, everything." If only I could secretly take a picture of his face and never have to listen to a single note come out of his mouth ever again.

Wait. A picture?

"Detective, why don't you ask Mr. Whatshisface over here some questions outside, it's such a beautiful morning."

The two men standing in front of me exchanged confusion for only a brief moment before Tom caught on. Finally, he was slowly stepping it up. Painfully slowly, but it was happening.

"Alright?" Mansplainer Man responded. (I think that was my favorite name for him.) As the two of them left the store from the main entrance and exit, it dawned on me that the security camera monitors could be under lock and key. Maybe not, but that would be just my luck.

Being the impatient person I am, I hopped over the counter even though the opening was about a few feet away. What can I say? I was tight on time. The back of the store was more like a backstage of a Broadway theater; open and organized, but still had a lot of crap.

Cameras, cameras, cameras. They had to be somewhere. Wasn't there some sort of law, or whatever? *Cameras, cameras, cam* - Suddenly, I heard a faint beeping. I didn't take as much pride in my hearing abilities as I did in my sense of smell, but my gifted ears did come in handy when Veena had her friends over and I hadn't been updated on the latest gossip.

It was getting louder, and it was coming from up - No, down! Below a table with a coffee maker and microwave, and right in front of my feet was a closed cabinet with no lock. Guess they weren't that precautious, but they *were* that stupid.

Sure as hell, the monitors were decently clear with updated security and labeled footage. A'ight, but man, this was gonna take a while. Luckily, everything was digital. I clicked on the home screen, went to the correct date and time, and pressed fast forward.

Okay, get your phone out and get ready to record.

"Okay, but I really should get back to -" I heard the small bell ring and the front door open. No, no, no, no, no. Mansplainer Man was coming back in. I flattened my stomach against the floor to hide myself as much as I could. Luckily, Tom wasn't completely useless.

"No, no, Sir. If you're not going to let us search your store, you owe us this much. Just a few more questions." Holy, moly. This kid was as dumb as a rock. He clearly never heard of the fifth amendment.

"Awkay, awkay."

Phew. Okay, almost there. I got to about one thirty, pressed record, and watched the few cars ride by, and thank God it was only a few.

One car, two cars, LOL, one guy's getting pulled over. Three cars...

Only two long minutes went by on fast forward and only a few pauses. Seven cars went by within the time frame that the police gave me, and I got them all on camera. Someone was going down.

Being as careful, and Harriet the Spy-like as I could, I crawled under the counter instead of hopping over it. Why? Honestly, I was just getting lazy. The boys must have been chit chatting away. Through the window I could see them laughing and nodding heads. Probably sports talk. Meh. Smart, Tom. Smart, but meh.

Not wanting Mansplainer Moron Man (I liked that addition.) to be suspicious, I acted like I stayed inside to do some casual shopping. With some M'nMs, root beer, and Ben and Jerry's, I knocked on the window, shook my items like I was seventy-six years old and there was no tomorrow, and the two new love birds frantically pranced back into the store.

After I asked Tom for some money to buy my snacks, we rolled on our merry way, and I filled him in on everything that I found.

"Not too many cars passed by within the time period that you gave me," I told the detective as we hopped in his car.

"Great. I can't believe this wasn't in the file already."

"Maybe nobody in the station knew they had cameras that pointed toward the roads."

"Maybe." A touch of hope filled his voice, but doubt outweighed it significantly.

"Good work, Detective."

In the most professional way, Tom firmly nodded his head, lifted the side of his mouth into a crooked smile, and said "Thank you. I appreciate it. So where am I dropping you off?"

"Staples."

PART 7: JULY 26TH, 2:57PM

The pictures were surprisingly cheap at Staples. I held them in my sweaty hands, but I should have put the pictures in a manila folder. The sweat awkwardly creased the paper. That only made paranoia shoot throughout my body and come out through my fingers and toes. I could not lose these pictures. Time was running out, I could just tell. And man, I really hoped that I wasn't gonna get caught.

After I passed under the bridge, to go into the other world, I ran to my mom's house. Veena wasn't there, and neither was my mom or Ralph. Probably at work. So I walked to my dad's house. She wasn't there either, and neither was my dad. Where the hell was she? This was usually the time that she was home. And an even bigger question, where was my dad? He worked nights. It was three in the afternoon. He should have been waking up by now, or in three to four hours. I could never really tell with that guy.

We got rid of the landline forever ago, and I was too afraid to use my own phone, so I decided the simple answer was to wait.

Nothing.

I waited for a solid seventeen minutes before my AHwhatever kicked in, and I felt like I was gonna die if I didn't do something or go somewhere. I at least needed to eat something.

Wait, I thought. *Of course. They all must be at the diner! Bernie's! I didn't know why my dad would be there too, but they must be having a special or something.*

My watch indicated to me that I was running out of time before my parents from the other world would notice that I was gone. The pictures needed to come, and I was going to have to randomly ask her about these cars at the dinner table. Man, my parents were gonna be pissed and weirded out at the same time. I crossed my fingers, hoping they wouldn't be paying that much attention to me tonight.

Bernie's was hopping. The lights outside were flashing like it was Christmas Eve, and there were no available parking spots in view. Even though there were barely enough parking spots for the staff and a single table in the first place. Highlights of living in a town the size of a pea, am I right? I could see both Dad's and Mom's car on the street. Why were they here together?

The second I opened up the door, the sound of off-pitch screaming overwhelmed my ears. Oh lord, karaoke night. Greeeeat. The song must have been a failure of the 80's because I am glad to say, I didn't recognize it.

It didn't take too long for me to find my family, but when I did, my heart crinkled into a raisin. Veena was laughing at one of my dad's horrible jokes. My mom looked healthy. She was still taking her anemia medication, which I was one hundred percent sure she forgot to take every night in my world. My mom and Lauren were chatting it up as if nothing had happened. Last time I saw Lauren, waiting on us, it was like her world had collapsed too.

Everything seemed back to normal. No pain. No sorrow. Just for a second, I imagined what would happen if I stayed here for the rest of my life. I hated myself for it, but selfishly, this was what I wanted more than anything in the world.

"Nov!" Veena screamed as she beckoned me over to their table.

My mother immediately began to interrogate me. "Where have you been, baby?" She screamed way louder than she needed to as I sat down.

"Um, I don't know." More self-beating was coming my way. I always felt bad after dodging my mom's questions when I didn't feel like thinking, but it always took too much energy out of me to respond to whatever I wasn't paying attention to.

"How ya doin', kiddo?" Kiddo. That's what my dad always called me. Original, right? Whenever he was in a good mood, which was usually only half the time, he would shout that name out with his thick Boston accent.

A few minutes passed by, that were probably more than just a few, before I gathered up the courage to talk to Veena. The more I thought about it, the more I felt like there were thick strings attached between me and my sister, but I was the one that put them there, and even worse, I was going to be the one that had to snip them.

"Heeey," I said as my overdue greeting to my sister.

"What's up?" Veena replied.

"Can I ask you something?" I didn't have time or the emotional capacity to exchange more pleasantries. I couldn't get more attached than I already was.

"Of course."

"So, this is gonna sound kinda weird, but can you look at these pictures and tell me if you remember any of these cars?"

"Cars?" Honestly, the fact that Veena knew less about cars than I did utterly escaped my mind. How did she drive so well? Wow.

"I know, I know, but I'm trying to find someone, and I know you have a really good memory."

"How exactly would looking at cars help?"

"I don't know...but I'm trying to find a cute boy."

"Oh my god. Let me take a look!" I didn't even have to reach out my arm and hand her the pictures. I knew that would get her going.

After putting on her pink reading glasses that she without a doubt didn't need, she inquisitively squinted at the photos as if I had just asked her to solve a quantum physics formula. Although I wasn't quite sure if those came in the formula form, but regardless, it looked like my so-called case breaking evidence wasn't gonna be useful after all.

"Sorry, dude," said Veena as she handed me back the now crinkled photos. "I don't recognize any of these cars, but they also aren't the best pictures. Where'd you get them?"

"Jack was taking pictures or something. I'm not sure. He's weird." I did prepare that answer ahead of time, but I gave her the lazy version just so I could change the subject. Nonetheless, she hesitantly nodded in agreement and drew her attention back to the cute drummer that had a red bandana on his head. Not my thing, but Veena was a Mötley Crüe fan.

I missed the way she looked at people. Being her little sister, it was always weird when I saw her make droopy, puppy eyes at boys. I don't know why, but I missed that weirdness. Even crazier, I missed the way she used to yell at me, and I would yell back at her. Anything that we did together, even though what we did was probably so stupid, like fight, or watch *Big Time Rush*. Man, that was a cringeworthy show. But I yearned to cringe over that show with her. Just one more time.

What I missed most of all, was how loving she was to my parents. I knew that they loved me just as much as they loved her, but ever since Veena died, I had such an overwhelming sense of protection towards them, especially my dad. He didn't have many people left in his life that he had a true connection with. He had a serious girlfriend for a while, but it didn't work out. Sarah was nice and all, but he just wanted to be a dad, and then, I was the only thing he had left.

Veena and my dad always had such a special "Daddy/Daughter" connection. She was Daddy's little girl. My dad and I were bros and all, but she made him laugh way more often than I ever did.

Like I've said many times before in my life, I did not grow up as a religious person. Although, I prayed to God that I never had to experience what it was like to lose a child, but then, I had almost a faint idea of what it's like to have a fraction of your soul ripped out of you. I was seeing it right then.

"Nov! Come dance with me!" Veena called out.

"Me? You've seen me at school dances, right?"

"Oh, come on. Suck it up, buttercup. We are about to have some fun!"

The sentimentality grew as the night went on, but in this moment, I didn't care that I didn't truly belong here. I didn't care that I knew I was gonna have to move on. I didn't care what was happening in my world at the moment. I was soaking up too much of my mother's love and warmth to care about the future. I had to see this as an opportunity. A gift. I got to see the light in my parent's eyes once more. Of course. I was never gonna be able to let that go, but I knew one day, I could make peace with it. I would be okay. Veena was going to consistently be teaching me just how to do that.

We danced for what only felt like five minutes, but apparently it was almost two hours. The music was insane. I had never felt the bass pulse so deep within my blood and bones. Veena probably just wanted to dance all cute for the drummer, and didn't wanna look like a loser so she dragged me along. But what are little sisters for if they aren't for that?

The love in my parent's eyes. They couldn't look away from us. It was another memory for the books that I would treasure forever, just for me.

Throughout the night, the drummer boy and Veena kept exchanging flirty glances. It pained me to know that she was never gonna get married or have any kids. She was the one that wanted those things, not me. She barely even got the chance to go on real dates, or have a nice, respectful boyfriend.

Into the night I sat and ate as much food as my stomach could possibly handle. My dad secretly gave me a few sips of his beer. If I had had any more, it sure as hell would have helped get all of the crap out of my stomach. Thankfully it didn't reach that point, but I knew for a fact that I was never going to drink as an adult.

After the band left and the diner stayed open for drinks and desserts, Veena and I chatted away. Only it was more than just simple chatting. This was my only chance to tell her everything I wanted to. There wasn't much left that I kept from her, but I wanted Veena to know everything, and I wanted to know everything about her. No secrets.

"Is there any other place that you would want to live outside of Connecticut?" I asked her. "Ya know, like after you graduate from Princeton and all?"

"Hey, I still haven't gotten into Princeton, remember? I can't plan anything like that just yet."

"Sure, you can. You must have at least a few ideas." Her face lit up as she smiled and stared at the floor. Her cogs were turning. I was right. She had a few plans up her sleeve.

"Honestly, I love Connecticut and all, but anywhere in the sun. Somewhere I can go to the beach year-round and my little puppies can play in the water. I still will never forgive Mom and Dad for not getting us a dog."

"They were getting divorced. What did you want from them?"

"All the more reason to get us a cute wittle puppy!" The laughter we exchanged was the purest thing I had felt in a while. I'd never locked a sound so deep into my brain before. "I also think I'm probably going to take a gap year before I actually go to Vet school." It took her a moment to actually look me in the eye. She stared into her glass of lemonade and hunched her back expecting a negative and aggressive response from me.

"Really?" I asked her, physically leaning into her timidness. "You were - I mean you're graduating a semester early so you can get to college as soon as possible. You don't wanna do the same for Vet school?"

"I honestly just wanna travel more. Remember that time we went to Spain right before Mom and Dad split? I think it's absurd that that is the only time I've been outside of the country. We've never even been to Canada. I'm desperate to explore. I'm not in any rush to make money, and with all the Vet schools that I want to apply to, I think they'd really admire my traveling experience if I took all of these massive trips."

Everything she said after that kind of blurred in my ear drums. Her need for traveling somehow gave me lightened comfort. I still wasn't sure if I believed in a "heaven" per se, but what if she could travel the world now just like she wanted? Maybe she was able to make her dreams come true. I knew right then that this would bring ease into my soul when I couldn't sleep at night, and maybe it could bring my parents some comfort too.

"So, who is this boy that you wanted to track down or something?" Veena suddenly asked me.

"Oh, this boy named Oscar." I surprised myself with how fast I came up with a fake name, I was just thrown off by the god-awful name, Oscar. *Really, Nova?*

"Sounds cute. Schoolboy?"

"Where else would I have met a boy?"

Suddenly, it occurred to me that it would be smart to ask her one more question. However, when I started thinking about the case again, lines of thick blood shot up my back and over my shoulders.

It's okay. You're here to help her. This is all for Veena. Stop overthinking it. Just breathe.

"If you wanted to find Orenth - I mean Oscar, what would you do?" I casually asked her.

"Well. If I were Raya, I would stalk him." I took a sip of my drink at the wrong moment, because my root beer float almost shot out of my nose from such staccato laughter. "You know it's true! But I would just maybe ask around and find out what car he drives, and you can follow him like a crazy woman. I mean, once you get your license. You know I got no time to drive you around even for a cute boy. Otherwise, you know I would."

Hearing her talk about her car made my blood feel even thicker as it continued to push up my spine, but then it slowly descended as two fingers snapped together in the back of my head.

Of course...Veena's car.

"Right. I need to look for more clues in the car."

"Clues? What?"

Man, I needed to stop saying things out loud. "Yeah, clues to get to him. You know. Sorry I'm just mumbling and making no sense." And I chugged my root beer float.

The night carried on, but I knew it was time to go home when I almost fell asleep at the table and even the overhead radio music in the diner was turned off. Lauren came back to our table to give us our check. She took some time to laugh with us and squeezed my hand before it was time to re-center myself and head home.

It was almost morning. Holy crap, Mom from my world was gonna kill me if she found out Jack was pretending to be me. Actually, I take that back. Jack was gonna be the one to kill me. He had literally been there for over twenty-four hours, probably still under the covers. Oh boy. Maybe he would go easy on me since I always kept snacks under my bed.

Veena and I said our good nights to our father, and headed home with our mom and Ralph. When we got home and the rest finally went to bed, I took my now way too common of a route and got ready to climb down the vines. But something twitched in my legs. They were having some sort of altercation with my brain who was telling me to get my ass to my world, but my legs were drawing me to the hallway and into my sister's room.

78

After a few moments of slowly walking, the only conclusion I could come up with was that the spirits of this world were reminding me to have one last look, just in case. I knew that I had to keep returning to this world until I solved Veena's case, but what if something happened? What if the bridge was destroyed or the magic ran out?

Quickly and quietly, I popped my head into my sister's dark room, and the small sliver of light brushed onto her olive skin and fake eyelashes. She looked so peaceful, similar to how I knew she was in my world now.

Slowly, I closed the door when I realized that if she opened her eyes, she would be hella freaked out. She was never an easy sleeper.

Surprisingly my feet had plenty of energy to fly me back to the bridge. As I zoned out, and let my taxi legs do their thing, I reviewed everything that happened this past night. Not about the case, but about my time with my sister. The peace I felt lingered, and I got over the tension that built in my body. I was strong enough to overcome it and brush it away for the important moments that I refused to have ruined. They were too precious. It was almost as if I was proud of myself, which didn't happen too often. All I could think was, I was growing. Even though I knew this wasn't my world, I was still becoming something other than Veena's annoying little sister.

The sun was almost out when I could see the bridge prominently standing in the morning dust. This was the journey that didn't make me afraid. Why would I be afraid to return to my own world? Of course, I never truly wanted to. I wanted to stay with my sister for the rest of my life, but it was my home. There was nothing scary about returning to where I belonged, but as my right leg swept through, a giant wave of resentment and grief slammed into my body. It was like the feeling was a gas that suddenly turned into a solid to wipe away my soul. After a second and a half of acknowledging the striking pain, I noticed that my breath had been completely ripped away, and instead of fighting to take another breath, I felt myself melting into the ground as my vision completely faded to black.

PART 8:
JULY 27TH,
8:20AM

Waking up by getting slapped in the face was a strange feeling. Let me break it down for you; First, your eyes open, and your vision focuses, but then, the pain in your face slowly crescendos into a mountain of stinging pain in your cheek. THEN you realize that you are still alive and finally conscious once more. It's an unfortunate, yet in this case, necessary incident.

"Nova!" Jack screamed for probably the thirtieth time. "Are you alright?"

It was just then that I realized that I also had a searing pain in my left arm, which was probably the arm that I had fainted onto. But regardless of that, I obviously answered, "Well, duh." Because that's how I always answered that question.

With just a little shake, my arm started to feel better, but Jack was already annoying me by taking all of my weight and pulling me up to a standing position.

"Does your head hurt?"

Obviously, my head hurt, but my chest, shoulders, and soul hurt a lot more. I wasn't sure how much longer I was going to be able to do this for. Going into the other world was like splashing Caribbean water on your face and rubbing it into your skin and hair. Everything radiated perfection, but no matter what, I had to keep convincing myself that it wasn't real, or at least it wasn't mine. This made coming back to my world all the more dreadful and remorseful.

"I - I miss my sister." Those were the first words that popped into my head, and thank God, Jack turned his embrace into a hug rather than keeping his cautionary stance as if I were eighty years old. I would have slapped him right back if he hadn't.

"I know. Me too. We all do, but none of us can imagine what you're going through. I know I've said this a million times, but I'm here for you anyways, and I believe you about everything."

I was still too dazed to process what he said right away, but when it came to me, I couldn't help but shake in his arms and let a single tear run down my face.

"Why is this happening to me?" Again, all I could do was let the words roll off my tongue. These were questions I hadn't asked yet, but I was so desperate for them to be answered. Although I was beyond fearful that they never would be.

"Because not everything about the universe makes sense, and that's the shittiest part about being alive."

Through all of the quivering, sobs, and clattering jaws, I absorbed every word that he said. This wasn't even close to the answer I was looking for, but it was an answer, and I knew one day, I would be at peace with it. Not today. Not soon, but one day. Just like everything else happening in my life.

"I need to get up," I cried into his shoulder.

"You are up, silly." He was right, but I was too oblivious to notice even after I heard him say it.

"I can't waste any time. I have a lead, or I have an idea."

"What do you need me to do?"

"I need you to come with me to the junkyard."

He didn't want to. My eyes were still blurry and fighting to catch a grasp on their focus and 20/20 vision, but they caught sight of Jack's eyes and in them was predicted resentment and tension. Regardless, he closed his eyes to breathe and said, "Of course. Do you really want to go right now? Do you want to call Detective Baron?"

"Yes. We can't waste time. And no. It's okay. We can do this on our own, and he would probably not approve. I already asked him to meet me at a random gas station hella early in the morning yesterday."

I couldn't remember the last time Jack had asked that many questions, but his concern and urge to be prepared and thorough brought me comfort that I'd been waiting for. Not that he owed me anything, but our friendship was one of the last solid relationships that I had. It needed to stay strong for both of our sakes.

"Alright. Let's go. What's the plan?"

It took us almost an hour and a half to get to the junkyard. From not knowing where it was, walking in the wrong directions and walking in general, time stacked a mile high. Even when we got there, we weren't sure it was the right place. Between the sketchiness, the lack of signs, and the multiple sections of broken fence we should have assumed it *was* the junkyard, but our lack of knowledge and familiarity with this part of town blocked our judgment.

"Is anyone working here?" Jack asked as we noticed no one sitting in what they probably called a booth. "There better be somebody working here. We did not walk all of this way to enter illegally."

After walking around for a few minutes, we finally came across a middle-aged woman wearing black, long-sleeved overalls, and headphones that were definitely from 1999. It looked like she was shoveling dirt to add something to the grounds, but she was certainly giving me some, *I'm hiding a body, don't look* vibes. Also, when she turned around with her drooping mouth, we could see she was missing most of her teeth. I knew it was a little rude to be thinking this, but *yikes!*

"Hello?" Jack yelled out to her. Nothing. "Helloooooo?"

I didn't have time for this. There was a wheelbarrow with tire parts to my right. My feet moved faster than my brain and subconscious, so with my strongish arms and heavy attitude, I rolled up my sleeves as I stomped over to the wheelbarrow and used every bicep curl I'd ever done to flip that beast over. Just like

I predicted, she ripped out her headphones and screamed at the top of her southern lungs.

"Hey! 'Nuff a dat! Whatchyall doin'?"

"We need your help." I asked as politely as I could.

"Why? What for? What's in it for me?"

"You don't even know what we were going to ask?" Jack never had a single drop of patience for people that were nowhere near as smart as him. That's why Veena always liked him so much, but I thought he was doing pretty well lately. Guess he had to start over.

"Fine. What y'all want?"

"I need to look at a car for evidence in a hit and run case. Please, it's really important." My, *Please let me have ice cream, Mom* voice was really starting to show.

"Y'all cops?" Crap. Maybe I should have brought Tom.

"No."

"Good. I hate cops. Come on in." Really? A southern woman with no teeth that was probably racist hated cops? That was a new one.

The woman beckoned us over into the car where at least fifty cars were stacked in surprisingly long aisles. This was already a lot easier than the gas station with Mansplainer Man, but it could've still taken a while until we found her car.

Apparently, they were organized in no particular order. So in other words; not organized. But thankfully, my senses tingled in a way that I had only felt in the other world. They were telling me to turn to the right and walk toward the tired sun that was hiding behind a few thick New England clouds. Somehow, my senses were right. Even though Jack was the one that found it, and my senses were telling me Veena's car was on the bottom of the stack, not the top, but close enough.

Below my sister's car was a red Jeep and a hatchback that looked like it was from the seventies. The car was way too high to see anything.

"Any way you could get it down?" I asked the woman that I was too afraid of to ask her name.

"You wan' me to get that car all the way up there down here?" Damn, she was already unimpressed.

"Yup."

"That'll be fifty bucks, cash."

No surprise there. I knew there had to be a catch. Now, here's the thing; of course, my sister was worth fifty dollars, but here's the other thing; I was fifteen goddamn years old, and I sure as hell looked like it. Jack even more so. How much money did this woman think I was carrying around?

"I don't have fifty dollars."

"Yeah, neither do I," Jack added.

"Then I guess I'll leave y'all here to figure somethin' out." And just like that the toothless woman lost the little bit of coolness I thought she had and strutted away from us.

"What do we do?" Jack asked, even though he was always the smart one with a plan.

"Hold my phone," I said as I threw him my phone and rolled up my sleeves.

"No. Absolutely not." It suddenly dawned on him that I was about to climb the cars. I guess the years of climbing the vines on the side of my house was about to come in handy in other rebellious parts of my life. "We're going to get caught." Nah. What was the woman gonna do? She left. I highly doubt she would have noticed or cared.

"Calm down. I'll be fine and quick."

The first car was easy. Jeeps were built with such muscular boldness, but climbing onto the hatchback, or whatever it was that people called it, was a little more challenging. Keep in mind, my doctor told me I was done growing and I was only about five feet tall, which, in this case, had its advantages. As in there wasn't much to pull up, but reaching to pull myself up in general was, no shit, a *challenge*. There also wasn't much to grab onto, so there was only one thing to do; jump.

"You're kidding me, right?" Jack had no business reading my mind, but he had the audacity to do it anyway. I didn't respond as I successfully flew into the air and grabbed onto the bottom of Veena's wheel. Welp. Didn't think that one through, 'cause there was nowhere to go from there. "Now what?" He continued to bug me.

"WOULD YOU SHUT UP ALREADY?" I searched around with my face in my armpit, and thank the heavens there was a rusty beam to my right. Carefully, but a lot quicker than I probably should have, I climbed over to it and immediately felt pieces of hard rust dig into my palms. The pain was difficult to ignore, but I shook it off by swinging my legs in between my arms and hooked them onto the beam. I was too scared to let go of the beam with my hands, but man did I want to. Instead I used all of the arm strength that I had left to pull myself onto my butt and I sat on the beam. Still, I wasn't sure how I was gonna get to the other side of her car, but this was a start. I freaking did it.

"Damn, girl."

"Dude, call up Tom Holland 'cause I think I found him a Spidergirl." I wasn't sure if that was even a character, but who cared? It was Tom Holland. Just as long as Jack never told him about that cringeworthy line.

"Just get down soon, so I can breathe again."

The light was terrible up there for some reason, but there was nothing in the car that I could see, except for...no I couldn't look. The blood stain was bigger than I thought it would be. After everything I'd been through the previous week, I thought for sure I would be able to handle this. Especially since my patience had been running scarcely low. The only thing that brought me comfort was knowing her soul hadn't left her body right in this vehicle. It was in the ambulance that rushed her to the hospital, but they were too late.

For some reason, I was feeling those weird senses again. Something was telling me to look down. Really? Look down? But the senses were also telling me to look down at Jack, he would know what to do. I did what I was told and squeezed onto the beam tighter than I already was and peered down below to see Jack's face telling me "You can do this." And somehow, that was all I needed.

I took one more glance inside the car, but nothing seemed out of order or straight up conspicuous. Everything in me had to fight the resistance to not think too much about how insanely dented the car was, especially when I looked deep and directly into those dents. Mindlessly, I scanned over the front dent a few times before I finally thought there was nothing there, but as I pulled my focus away, I had to do a double take as I noticed something odd. Something small that the police probably didn't see.

"Is that a -" I mumbled to myself as I squinted my eyes to get a better look at a small, well very small, black streak of car paint. Car paint! Holy Bejesus. The car that hit her was black! It didn't seem like much, but from what I could remember, two of the cars that I found on the security cameras were black. Man, this could be it.

"THE GODDAMN CAR WAS BLACK!"

"OH, HELL YEAH!" Jack screamed back in support. I had the best friend in the entire world. Everybody needed a Jack in their life.

I took a few pictures of the black streak and the entire car with the license plate so it would be solid evidence. I've never gripped my phone so tightly in my entire life.

Climbing down was surprisingly easier than I thought. I assumed I would be much more graceful about it, but Veena got Mom's gymnastics genes, and I got Dad's basketball legs. Finally, I took my last tumble onto the ground and fell onto my hands and knees as I plunged into the dirt.

"Jesus, are you okay?"

"I'm more than okay. We're gonna catch this son of a bitch."

The internet was pretty useless when it came to searching how many people owned black Honda Accords and black Camrys in the area. When I got back home that night, I cracked down to work and got the least amount of sleep I had in over two weeks. The images were too low quality, and the street was too far away from the camera to get any license plate number, but I still had hope. I had to.

At probably seven in the morning, my arms and back gave up, and they shriveled into a pile of goo on my desk as I lost complete control over them. It was as if someone had a remote control to my body and I was a robot that was losing battery power. Rare was the day that I actually felt still as a rock when I was falling asleep, but unfortunately, I was interrupted by a goddamn Mariachi band.

"HAPPY BIRTHDAY TO YOUUUUU, HAPPY BIRTHDAY TO YOUUU!"

Shiiiit. I mean, asking myself how I forgot my birthday would be a stupid question, but damn I felt bad about how terrified my face looked when my mom came in with a halfway decent smile on her face for the first time in weeks. Mom, Dad, Ralph, and Jack probably put all the effort they had left into their little surprise.

"Happy birthday, baby," my mom quietly cried out as though to remind me. She probably could tell I was more than just shocked.

"Thank you, guys!" I managed to spill out of my throat, still slapping myself in the face.

"We know you don't like big surprises, Nova," Ralph added, "so we thought we would just do a little show for you."

"At..." I looked at the clock just in case it was noon, and I was just being a lazy buttface, "...8:45 in the morning?" Turns out I was being reasonable in my questioning.

"You're usually an early riser, Nova. What do you mean? I hear you walking around at six in the morning all the time."

Whoops.

"Happy sweet sixteen," Jack finally spoke, even though he knew I hated the idea of a *sweet sixteen*. I was excited to drive and all, but that's about it. What else happened? I could legally have sex or something? Yeah, that wasn't gonna happen anytime soon.

"No," I snapped back at him, "but thank you. I really appreciate it."

"We have cake for later, kiddo," said Dad with a little more excitement than his beer belly should be asking for. "Although, I do have something for you now."

Oh lord. What were they gonna give me? This sounds like probably the strangest thing about me, but I kind of hated getting presents. They were always crappy, I never used them, and I was the least materialistic person on the planet. I don't know why, but I hated having stuff.

"Say hello...to Charles," and just like that, my dear old dad ran to the hallway to pull out the most beautiful mountain bike I'd ever seen in my life. Ohhhhhh this was actually gonna come in quite handy. Nice one, Dad.

"Oh my GOOOOOD, thank you, thank you! But we are absolutely not calling it Charles!" I wrapped my arms around him so tightly I didn't even think about thanking the rest of them. My guess was they probably all chipped in. Money was gonna be tight for at least the next few months because of Veena's funeral costs, but I was about to tell them they could make this my birthday present for the rest of my life.

"We're so glad you like it," my mom smiled. The ease in her eyes was so prominent at that moment. Seeing your child as happy and excited as I was after such a tragedy must have such a strong, consoling power to it. This only made me more excited.

"You guys didn't have to bring it in. I could have come down." To be real, I didn't hear what anyone said next because I was too busy admiring the stunning red paint perfectly displayed across it. "I love it, thank you."

I hadn't had a bike since I grew out of my first one, which took a looooong time. The warmth from the room seeped into my skin. I almost forgot Veena wasn't in this world anymore, which almost led me to say something along the lines of, "I can't wait to tell Veena!" But thank almighty Jesus that I shut that wide mouth of mine up. However, I was in fact hella anxious to tell Veena.

I'd never been *completely* obsessed with my birthday. Don't get me wrong, birthdays have always been great fun. From what I could remember, I usually got what I asked for, which was money ninety-nine percent of the time, and friends always showed up. And of course, when I say, "friends" I mean Jack. I'd never been too needy, and it was easier to keep the list short. I'd never been the tiara-wearing, "WHERE'S MY PONY?" kinda girl either. Now, I'm thankful that I wasn't. It would have made my birthday even harder without my sister. Especially since I knew this had to be my last birthday with her, and it wasn't even in my own reality. It felt different, but it was something.

I dropped my new bike before my feet stumbled more than usual while walking down into the empty stream. The soil was drier and my legs grew unsteady. Eye twitching wasn't usually a problem for me, but looking past the under part of the bridge made every nerve and blood vessel in my body stop and scream. They wanted to remind me how passing through this portal was altering the flow of my soul, and it would do nothing but get worse. The last time I passed under this bridge, I passed out from the painful reminder that my sister was, once again, gone. Just gone. I hadn't passed through this barrier too many times yet, but I'd already lost count, and the incline of the pain levels was dramatic. This is what I had to do for both me, and for Veena.

An instigative, yet damaging thought shivered through my head. What were Veena and I going to do for my birthday? It's not like I could show her my new bike, but we could go for a canoe ride instead? Whatever it would be, I wanted to do something that *she* was craving to do. It didn't matter to me what we did, I just wanted to see her smile with pure joy in her eyes. And then after, when I returned to my own world, I could tell her all about it...at her grave. It was time. It was time to visit her a while ago.

Somehow, knowing that I could still communicate with her in my own way in my own world gave me the courage to pass through the portal under the bridge, and it felt amazing. How psychotic and messed up is that?

After the euphoric feeling, I sensed a little nausea in my stomach. Kind of like after jumping on a trampoline, or swinging on a swing. However, I did nothing, but laugh, because of course, I felt a little queasy. That's just how my life went. If I'm being real, I was kinda getting used to it. My confidence was growing to the point where I thought I could get through anything.

My peaceful walk back to my house left me more tired than before. God only knew why I could possibly be tired after being woken up by screaming, off-pitch family members at the crack of dawn, but the second I opened the door, Veena's face was inches away from mine.

"There you are! HAPPY BIRTHDAAAY!"

After she hopped on me like a rabies-infected rabbit, and jumped on me like an oddly tall toddler, I was up for anything.

PART 9: JULY 29TH, 4:49PM

Thank God, Dad bought me this bike for my birthday. Running was aging me fifty percent faster than I was supposed to be. Besides, biking was peaceful. Thoughts floated around just a little bit easier, and didn't just stick to the side of my skull. Although, it made my ride to the graveyard way too fast. I didn't have enough time to prepare how I was gonna go about this.

Maybe I should have asked Jack to come with me. He probably would have said, "I'll go, but you should do this on your own," since that's the kind of person that he's always been. But even just having his hand to hold before I approached Veena's grave on my own. That would have made everything just...better. Instead, I reread his encouraging text and held the phone to my chest.

You can do anything. You know that, right?

After all, I did pass back through the portal without passing out the other day, which was an improvement from the time before. Although, I wasn't sure which was gonna be more painful; reentering a world where my sister didn't exist after doing so multiple times, or actually acknowledging it and seeing her name on a grave.

It took them a while to finish her headstone, so my parents only came here for the first time last week. I'm still beating myself up for not going with them, but I think they understood that I just wasn't ready. However, there was a sense of pride that sprouted within me when I told myself it was time to see her all on my own. Nobody really had to bug me to do it. I just knew.

The map that the church person gave me wasn't up to par, but that was mainly because I was directionally challenged and probably needed glasses. It took me a while to find her stone in the three-acre graveyard, but when I did, I suddenly looked up from the map, and it was just...there.

This was for sure not the moment that my sister's death "hit me". Like I said, it already slammed right into me quite a few times. But this...it seemed so out of place, like it was a screwed-up joke that we had together.

If I didn't walk right up to her headstone, I was going to make a run for it, screaming and crying. So, I laid my bike to the ground, pulled the roses out of my backpack, and stood precisely five feet away from the brown stone that said, "Veena Cressida Rosa...Daughter, Sister, Friend."

In my opinion, they should have added some pretty quote that reflected her life, but Veena probably would have slapped someone upside the head and said, "That's cheesy, ya dork" or something along those lines.

After I gently laid the roses right in front of her name, I stood there unable to even think of what to say. I didn't wanna think. I just wanted to be with my other half for a while in my own world and mumble away with whatever crappy improvisation skills that I pulled from my ass. Veena would have loved it.

"Hey, dork," I began. "Sorry that was mean. I don't know how to greet you any other way though. To be honest, I blame that on you, and a little bit on Raya too. I saw her the other day, ya know. She talked to me and was probably the kindest she's ever been in her life. Turns out you have an effect on people even if you aren't physically here."

"So, I should tell you...there's this place. I don't know what it's called. I don't know how it got there, but I do know that you're there. Yeah, I know. *You're* there, and I know why it's there. It sounds insane, but I'm the only one that can travel in between these two worlds. Does that even make sense? That's how I know it was built, or created, or something like that so I can find peace. It's there for me to be able to say goodbye to you, and that comes with finding out who did this to you.

"You should have seen the look on Jack's face when I told him. He tried to pretend to believe me, because of course he did, but he definitely didn't. Not at first. Now he does because apparently, he saw me pass out when I came back through the portal under the bridge. Oh yeah, by the way, that bridge that you always used to find me sitting on all upset when we were younger, that's the bridge that has the portal thing in it. All I have to do is walk under it. And get ready cause this sounds even crazier. There was this deer. I think it hypnotized me or influenced me or something to walk under that bridge. It was almost like you sent her to give me a message or something.

"Speaking of which. For some reason I gave a lot of thought as to why that portal is where it is. I think it's because that was always the place where you came the closest to...I guess saving me. You always figured out a way to make everything okay. Even when we were little, and now it's my turn to save you.

"It's going pretty well by the way. The case. Detective Baron is cool, and he's the only one I can trust on the force. Also, I'm really glad you have a nice spot in the cemetery. The trees are really nice in this area. It'll be nice in the springs and falls when I come here. Maybe we could have a day every week when I come by? Like a little sister date - Sorry, no, that's weird. Why would I call it that? Maybe I'll just call it 'Nova and Veena Time'. Yeah. I think that's cute. I mean we had names for everything, right?

"Hey, I have an idea. Why don't you help me name my new bike? She's red and beautiful. At least I feel like she's a 'she'. Dad and Ralph wanted to name her 'Charles', but don't worry, I shut that down right away. You were always pretty good at naming things. I bet you're naming all of your flowers right now. Wherever you are. What about Cressida? I was always jealous of your middle name. Thank you for never rubbing Ruth in my face, by the way. I'm still not sure where Mom and Dad even got it from. But

Cressida...It's stunning. I can't remember what it means, but still. Cressida. It suits her.

"Also, Mom's doing surprisingly well. She's actually sleeping through the night. Dad would be doing better if he wasn't so lonely. I promise I'll go over his house more, and I'll work on finding him a girlfriend. I'm sure he'd fail miserably on those dating apps, so I gotcha...or I got him. You - you know what I mean.

"Sorry. I know I'm not like - I'm just trying to make this as normal as possible. You know I'm not good with change and stuff like that, but obviously it's so much more. This...it's just a change that I don't know if I'll ever be able to handle. I was always so happy to see you. Even when I was pissed at you. But I'm not sure if 'happy' will ever be the word to describe me seeing you here. Though I want it to be so bad.

"I just really need you here to tell me what to do. About everything. You were always the leader, and when I ever tried to be the leader you would always yell at me and tell me to calm down or cut it out. I'm not sure I know how to do this without you. I keep screwing up and going in the wrong direction, and I'm so afraid that everything will get so bad, and you won't be here to fix it or help me.

"This other you, in this other world. It's not that she doesn't feel real. It's that the world doesn't feel real. I know that because I feel you with me all the time. Sometimes I miss you so much that I feel - I feel like I can't breathe. I hope that one day coming here will remind me that you really are with me all of the time. I know you. I know that you'll never leave my side, ever.

"Literally nonstop I've been thinking about what it's like where you are. If you're safe. If you're comfortable or okay? I guess it's my turn to worry about you. Sometime...would you let me know somehow that you're okay? I just want to tell Mom and Dad that you are. We all just need to know.

"I'm sorry if you can't hear me well. I knew I was gonna cry. It's not like I'm stupid or anything, but - sorry I'm just mindlessly talking. Though I know you're used to me doing that and all.

"I'm not sure what else I should say. It might be like this for a while. Me just monologuing to you about random things passing through my head. What else are sisters for, right? God, I really miss calling you that. I'm afraid that I won't be using that word as often. That can't happen, I won't let it. Even if I annoy the living crap out of everyone around me. I want to keep calling you my sister as much as I can, Veena. Because if there's one thing I know. I'm never ever going to be an only child."

When I finally laid down on the dirt that hadn't grown any grass yet, I realized how tired I was of crying. When was it going to stop? When was I going to be able to breathe like a normal human being again? I wasn't looking for an end to the suffering, I was looking for the capability of coping with the suffering. Nobody was making me feel as if I was going to get through this. I know Jack was trying, but so far it just wasn't working. Mom was bumbling by, on her own, and Dad almost seemed like he was shoving it all down. There was no reassurance from anyone, especially me.

What if I never found the person responsible? What if I went completely mad and refused to stay away from the world that wasn't mine, or stay there permanently in a false reality? I would never be able to move on. There would always be a hole there that would keep getting bigger and rustier.

I might have fallen asleep after a while, but I wasn't sure. The dirt was warm and surprisingly more comfortable than I thought, but something did spark my attention. A noise. A car door slamming.

"Ah, crap!" I heard a man yell.

My body shot up without even thinking. My deaf ears could tell at first where it came from, but it was just...odd. Nobody really ever came here, or at least I'd never seen anyone here while driving by. And besides, I thought cars weren't allowed to come into the cemetery.

At first, I didn't see anyone or a car, but a giant gravestone that stood at least twelve feet tall blocked my view of the south side of the cemetery. Multiple voices in the back of my head told me to look past the gravestone, but to also, and more importantly, be careful.

I ducked down not realizing it probably wasn't gonna do anything, but when I walked over and peaked out from behind the gravestone, I saw that my suspicions were correct. The ugliest green car faced my direction, and if I squinted my eyes, the person in the car had either the thickest, darkest eyeglasses in the world, or they had binoculars. Either way, I was beyond positive that they were staring straight at me.

I was careful to not be seen, but apparently not careful enough. Probably two seconds after I caught sight of the car, they drove off. And when I say, "drove off", I mean they made a big mistake by plunging their foot into their gas pedal and left the scene.

If they casually drove by with binoculars, my dumbass would have probably said something like, "Oh they're just taking in the view of these dead woods that has a shed from the 1950s that desperately needed a paint job. And right now, they just happen to be looking at me." Sometimes I could be really thick, what can I say?

But driving off like that really sent goosebumps popping up all over my arms and legs, until a realization made my goosebumps almost explode.

"Wait," I said aloud. "I've seen that car before." The mark on the left side of the car made it unmistakable. It looked like an alligator dipped its tail into black ink and slapped it across the side. I just couldn't remember where I'd seen it before.

Think, Nova, think.

I pulled a full Jimmy Neutron and shut my eyes so tight, they almost shot out of the back of my head. Luckily, I remembered before that could actually happen.

"Oh. My. God." I saw that car at the police station. The first time I went. It was the day after the funeral. Maybe whoever hit my sister was arrested that day for something else. Wait...no. That didn't make any sense. Why would somebody drive to a police station if they were arrested? Wouldn't a cop - *No.*

Everything in my mind went blank. Just like when I first learned of my sister's death. I couldn't wiggle my fingers or my toes. I could barely even blink. Could that be possible? What if a cop hit my sister? That would explain...*everything.* The black paint on my sister's car. The police car driving by in the video I took from the gas station. The blue piece of glass I found. Why Captain Sanders barely wanted to touch my sister's case. She was probably covering for them.

This whole time I thought a cop could be covering for their kid or someone they knew. Why would they be following me and not avoiding me if they didn't want to risk exposing their kid? Whoever they were, they probably thought I was onto them. Little did they know, they just made my job so much easier, because I sure as hell was.

I needed a plan, and fast. I couldn't show my face anywhere. These people knew what I looked like and were stalking me. I needed a disguise, so I could find out who this person was.

Although, cops usually travelled in twos. Holy crap. I was probably looking for two people. Right! The footprint on the passenger's side of the car! Two dirty cops. This town had already been through enough losing Veena. I wouldn't be surprised if they started a riot after I identified these cops.

If only that surveillance system was from the twenty-first century, I might be able to figure out who the cruiser belonged to. Or at least Tom would be able to. Oh, crap. What was Tom gonna think? He was gonna lose his mind hearing this. This couldn't be a text or phone call discussion. I needed to tell him in person, but first I needed to search through Veena's closet and look to see if she kept that blonde wig from her Legally Blonde Halloween party.

PART 10:
JULY 30TH,
1:06PM

When I get impatient or antsy, I usually go for a walk. So I did...up the staircase of the police station, and back down again. To be fair they were decently steep. Somewhat of a calming workout right there. Looking at the clock was just gonna make everything worse. It would also distract me from keeping my eye on the car. I had no time for my AHwhatever today.

Whenever someone came down the stairs, I would pull my cap down over my face even farther than it already was. It definitely wasn't gonna make a single difference, but whatever. I was already wearing a wig, and not one, but two of Veena's push up bras. So now I was basically Malibu Barbie. Not a single person was gonna recognize me, but the natural paranoia hadn't lessened in the past few weeks. Clearly.

After what was probably around an hour and a half, a few people came out of the station and waited on the steps a few feet away from me. They were quiet with glumness seeping out of their faces. They were probably waiting for information on something or someone. My impatience inclined as I was hoping one of them would get into the suspect's car, but all three of them barely even moved.

Jesssuuuus, I thought, until I realized that this could probably be of use to me. Perhaps having other people randomly hanging out on the steps of the police station might make me look a little less conspicuous. I had to remember, whoever was in that car knew who I was and was following me. However, all of that was unnecessary when Tom came storming down the stairs.

"Nova?" The detective called out to me. At first, I played it cool and assumed he only suspected it could be me but nothing in his mind was confirmed. Standing there and ignoring him seemed like the most logical option. "Nova, I know it's you. You forgot to cover up the distinctive mole below your cheek."

Wow. He was definitely a better detective than I thought.

"Sorry," I said as I turned around and dipped my sunglasses over the tip of my nose. "Should I explain?"

"Why do you think I came out here?"

Okay, better detective than I thought, but still needed some work 'cause he was about to blow my cover with his volume and tone.

"Fair point." I told him my whole theory and the evidence to back it up. It took some convincing since there could have been multiple versions of this car driving around, but I reassured him that the distinct, black, curved mark on the side of the left door and bumper was unmistakable. That was the car that was following me.

"Wow." That's all he said for a few intense breaths while looking at his messy shoe laces. "Just - wow - um. You really think it's someone at the station?"

"I don't think it's just someone at the station, Detective. I think it's a cop. Remember I saw that cruiser pass by on the security cameras? I didn't think anything of it, but then I saw this car following me, AND there was black paint on Veena's car."

"Wait. How do you know that?"

"I really wouldn't ask that question if I were you."

Tom used his palm to rub in between his eyebrows for way longer than any human being should in my opinion. Even when he was talking, it was like he was the one being interrogated.

"Alright, here's what we're going to do. You will wait here to see whose car that is. I think it's safer than me trying to get past the security in the station. So wait here while I go and see if I can find any evidence of cruisers that need repairing or were just recently repaired. Sound good?"

"I don't know, I'm sixteen." He had no idea how long I had been wanting to say that, because seriously. What the hell did I know? But yes, it sounded good.

"Right, okay. I think it's a good plan, so yeah. Let's do it. Call me when you see something, or I'll call you."

I gave him a two-fingered salute, and he walked back up the stairs. It wasn't until Tom swung the entrance door open that I realized I hadn't been keeping watch on the car except for when I pointed it out to him.

"Dammit!" I loudly whispered to myself as I whipped my body around so fast I almost took a graceful tumble down the stairs. I say graceful because my two padded bras probably would have protected me.

All of the air slowly escaped my lungs as my eyes caught sight of the car still there, sitting in the bright, late lunchtime light. But in the corner of my left eye, two men were walking towards the ugly green car. They were out of uniform, but I recognized them. They were two officers that I saw when I went to yell at Sanders either the first or second time. (Had there been a third? At this point I couldn't remember.)

The taller one was blonde with a creepy mustache and the other had a hella patchy goatee. Both wore deeply worn-in hiking boots, and ripped up flannels. The two of them stopped right in front of the car, but looked at each other as if they were announcing a loved one's tragic death to the other. If I squinted, I could see their mouths moving, but they could have been chewing gum while staring at each other for all I knew. Just when I was about to slowly walk up and maybe get a hint at what they were about to do next, Patchy Man opened the door to the green, ugly ass car and sat in the driver's seat.

I knew it.

Before this, I hadn't had much shortness of breath. In the past few weeks, it had mainly been lumpy throats, swollen eyes, wrinkly face, and tense shoulders, but now I just wanted to scream and punch a hole through these concrete stairs like Thor with his hammer. It felt like forever since my sister was killed, and now I finally found out who did it. It had to be him. Now all I needed was why, and how it happened. Maybe those two things were the same in a way, but I had to know every single little detail if I was gonna go to Sanders for this, including if both of these partners were in on it or just Patchy Man. Wait. No. Was Sanders in on this? I had to figure that out too.

Both of the men got in their cars and drove away before I scrambled for my phone to call Tom. Turns out Veena's knock off purse was too big and had too much crap in it for me to find anything, but when I reached for it, Tom was already calling.

"You found something already?" I asked in shock.

"You know the cruisers are right on the other side of the building, right?"

"How on earth would I know that?" I don't know, Nova. maybe because they were right outside out in the open? Dumbass. Jesus, why did I say that?

"Never mind. You were right. Cruiser 641 has new paint on it, but it was a crappy job and there are still some blue streaks on the white paint, but they're small. They probably did this in a hurry."

"How did they repair it without anyone noticing?"

"They probably didn't need much work done. Police cruisers are built like tanks."

All I could think was, *Man, police departments either have budgets that were way too big or have whacked out budget plans, but probably both.*

"Who's they?" I asked. "What are their names?"

"Right now, 641 is registered to Officers Stanley Rickers and Ken Smith. Smith is a newbie, and Rickers is a transfer from New York. Lieutenant Barry brought him in, I think. But Rickers has been kind of giving me the creeps the past maybe six months, I think, that he's been here. And don't even get me started on Smith. He's as dumb as a rock, he makes me look like James Bond."

Hearing Tom beat himself up like that made me feel ashamed that I ever gave him crap behind his back, but apologies needed to come later.

"Which one has a mustache, and which one has a patchy goatee?" I asked him.

"Uhhhh, how do you know that?" It had now officially dawned on me that I hadn't told him my good news.

"Oh, right. I just saw them leave in that hideous green car. The one with the patchy beard was driving it. The other one left in an SUV."

"Patchy guy is Smith." Of course he was. "Are you absolutely sure about this, Nova? You could get in some deep shit for accusing even one police officer of manslaughter, but two?"

I had never heard him swear before, but it made me feel more confident in his work on this case. He was toughening up.

"I have never been more positive about anything." That wasn't true, but I just knew I couldn't be wrong, and I was going to prove it.

Tom texted me their police headshots, which looked more like Halloween mugshots, but I just prayed that Veena recognized them from somewhere, anywhere. And I prayed that my phone would work in the other world since I didn't have time to go to Staples, and I hadn't fully tested it yet.

I texted my mom while I took the bike to the bridge since I had three missed calls from her, and I forgot to call back after all of them. Nothing could interfere with this. I needed to be at 100%.

On the other side of the bridge, I immediately checked my phone. Got it. Still had the pictures. Thank God. I texted Veena to ask for her whereabouts, and what-do-ya-know? She was, of course, at Raya's. To my surprise, I didn't have a bad taste in my mouth about Raya. In my world, things were good with us. At least for now. She was growing into a more kind-hearted human being, and she didn't deserve my temper. So I lied and told Veena that I was puking and desperately needed Gatorade. It took some pleading, and a few more lies about the color of my puke, but after about a half an hour of pathetic begging, she finally gave in. Because of course she did.

"Fine. I'll be right there." Usually she wasn't more aggressive than that.

She took her damn sweet time, but after she saw that I was indeed up to par in my health standards, I really couldn't blame her.

"Nov, you don't look sick."

"Well, I'm not feeling my best, but I just really wanted you to come home." Ohhhh boyy. She looked at me like I just told her that Tom Brady had left the Patriots.

"What? Why?" Her vocal cords must have been doing gymnastics in her throat. "What do you want?"

"Okay, don't kill me, but also please don't ask any questions."

"What's that supposed to mean?"

"Have you seen these men before?"

One of Veena's biggest pet peeves was when people didn't answer her questions. The audacity of doing so made her feel irrelevant. Personally, I didn't blame her, but I did give her a special request of not asking any questions.

She brushed her annoyance to the side for the time being and looked at the pictures on my phone with a cocked chin still planted in her jaw, but it quickly faded away when she looked deeper into the chilling photos.

"Actually, I think I do."

I'll be damned, that was the last thing that I was expecting.

"Veena, this is so important. You won't understand. I mean, maybe you will. Maybe someone will tell you one day, but I can't right now. I need you to think harder than you ever have in your life, and I know that's pretty damn hard. Where do you recognize these men from?"

"They're these two officers that have been stationed at the same spot for probably months now. You know that gas station that's on my way to work? They park their police car maybe a few hundred feet away from it. They pulled me over one time for seriously going the exact speed limit and told me to go over like everyone else. They're *those* kinda cops. I actually think they were chasing someone the other day. I don't know how long it lasted, but I saw them pull out of their sad spot and turn on their lights."

There it was. I had the answers I needed. These idiot cops lost control of the wheel, or they weren't paying attention and hit my sister when they were on a speed chase. In this world, they missed. That was the only difference, and it made me get really philosophical for just a fraction of a second. If only that were the truth. Just a few feet over, or a glance up a second sooner, and it would have changed my life. It would have saved my soul. My sister would still be in my world.

A single tear fell down my cheek before I quickly hid it away. This tear was a peculiar one. The emotional drop of water was a mixture of relief, grief, sadness, and just a touch of warmth. I don't think happiness was the right word, but the warmth just made me feel closer to Veena, even though a version of her stood just a few feet away from me.

"Listen," I started up again. "I need to prove these guys did something. They did something absolutely horrible." By the way she hesitantly opened her mouth, she was probably about to ask what they did, but in Veena fashion, she kept her composure.

"There's got to be video evidence if they did this on the job. Cops have to wear body cameras and cruisers have cameras too, and if they deleted it, that's also substantial evidence since it's pretty suspicious." Of course she knew all of this.

"Wouldn't somebody notice if the feed was missing?"

"Probably not. That's a lot of footage for each station to look at. I don't think they would go through it unless they needed to."

Right at this moment, I'd never been more grateful that Detective Tom Baron existed. All he had to do was get that footage.

"Veena, you're a genius." I hugged and kissed her on the cheek as she kept her confused stance and facial expression.

"Wait, wait," she snapped, stopping me from leaving. "Are you being safe?" The way she said the word, *safe*. It came so naturally to her. I missed how she would obnoxiously look after me.

"Yeah, of course."

"I know that I said I wouldn't ask any questions, but these are cops. Do you understand what you're getting yourself involved in?"

Holy moly, she had no idea. Of course, I knew what I was getting involved in. I was the *only* person who knew what I was getting involved in. Well, I guess besides the officers involved.

"Yes, of course. Don't worry. I'll be back later." As much as I wanted to stay with my sister, my anxiety about putting these men behind bars was driving my feet out the door full force, but Veena wasn't done.

"Come on, Nova. You have to tell me something."

"No, I actually don't." I didn't mean to snap at her like that, but it just came out. Damn it. I hated having this tension between us.

"Do you not trust me or something?"

"What? No, I'm just...protecting you?" The low confidence and skeptical tone I put into my voice was definitely a mistake.

"Oh, real-"

"Would you just stop treating me like a little kid for once?" This time, I think I meant to snap at her. "You don't always have to be this ridiculous idea of a perfect sister that just makes everything harder in one way or another!"

Saying that convinced me that I had zoned out for a minute, like it almost didn't happen. Then again, nothing seemed real anymore. Especially in this world. I guess this was something in the back of my head that I'd been wanting to say to her for a while now, but it just seemed stupid now that I said it. Being Veena's obnoxious little sister finally made me snap.

"Fine," Veena mumbled, the way girls always do when they are absolutely not fine.

"I'm sorry," I responded, shrugging my shoulders.

"Don't - I -" The way that she turned away from me, biting her nails tweaked my shoulder and chest muscles at the same time.

This was probably how most sisters usually fought, but Veena was always the one to say something along the lines of, "Hey, what's going on? How do we fix this?" when an argument began between us. Whoever, or whatever, gave me this opportunity of coming to this world to see my sister again was definitely not pleased with me at the moment, but this had to wait. What if these officers had seen me and they were halfway to Canada?

"Well, I'm sorry anyways," I firmly stated before I walked out the door.

My usual reaction to our altercations was an intense amount of eye rolling or hysterical laughter because a lot of our arguments originated from me stealing her clothing and then telling her my reasoning was because it looked better on me. But the moment I walked out the door and realized I was returning to a world where she didn't exist, while she was probably thinking less of me, I couldn't help but crouch down for just a moment and release the tension in my face to cry.

This wasn't how it was supposed to happen. This wasn't how *anything* was supposed to happen, but that's just how my life went. Nova Rosa, the loser that always messes everything up and can't do anything right. Even when I'm given the chance to make things right, I mess it up again. I knew I had to be right about these officers, but putting them behind bars was going to be a whole other undertaking.

PART II:
JULY 30TH,
7:32PM

So, let's recap; In the past few weeks, I've lost my sister, found the entrance to another dimension, found my sister again in this new dimension, illegally recorded security footage, probably illegally climbed a junkyard stack of cars, snuck out of my house multiple times, lied to my parents, alienated my sister, and now I was about to head to the police station to put away two cops for manslaughter. Or at least I hoped I was about to, or else there would be what my dear old mother liked to call, "Baby Poppin". This was when she would threaten to pop me and my sister's heads off if we didn't stop fighting. Who in the hell knew how I would pop anyone's head off, but I'm a creative person. These people needed to take responsibility for what they did, but more so, I needed closure.

    Funny...I mean it wasn't funny at all, but rather peculiar. There was nothing that I wanted more than to find out who did this to Veena, and to just move on with my parents, but now that it was about to happen, I felt a hint of resentment slide up my throat.

It's time to move on, I kept repeating to myself. *It's time to move on.* Moving on meant staying in my world. That was the only way I could accept the true reality. This was my world. This was real. I was about to storm into the police station and tell them exactly what happened to my sister, because that's what really happened, not what happened in the other world.

If someone poked their grimy hands into my chest and ripped out my heart, they wouldn't be able to tear it into smaller pieces. Whatever remained would simply fall through their fingers. If that's the way it had to be, I might as well use that while putting these men away.

"NOVA!" I heard behind me. That voice would stand out to me in a goddamn baseball stadium. I turned around to see Jack running like a chicken across the parking lot.

"What are you doing here?" I asked him.

"Detective Baron got a hold of me. He only told me to make sure you were okay, but I figured I would try and help you out."

"You knew I was gonna be at the police station like at this very moment?"

"No. I've been following you since your house. You're just a lot faster than me." Actually, I think a chicken would be faster than this boy.

"Oh. Well what exactly did the detective tell you?" He continued to tell me that Tom had filled him in on everything. The evidence we had, what we were going to present to the Captain, and our suspicions on how the Captain could possibly be involved.

"Don't you think you should look for more evidence before accusing the Captain as well?"

"No. That's the whole point. That's my plan. We need to see how she reacts to this evidence. What we have, all this information, it warrants more than an arrest. It all *has* to convict them. It HAS to! All we have to do is catch her in a lie...or something like that. We should probably leave that up to the detective though."

We proceeded up the stairs. Jack had to give my hand and my shoulder a little squeeze before we went in, but all I could think was; *This is all for you Veena. You'll have your vengeance. Your justice.*

With my height, clothes, and slightly high-pitched voice, I had to stay strong. These people needed to feel my power, but more importantly my anger.

"You ready?" Jack asked me before he opened up the front door.

"As ready as I'll ever be."

The station was busy today. Not sure why. They definitely weren't scrambling to figure out who had done this to Veena, but the busier the better. I wanted people to see this.

"Excuse me, Captain Sanders!" I called out to her as I saw her talking to her lieutenant. When I say that she made it blatantly obvious that she wasn't happy to see me, I mean she probably would have rather had Ted Bundy casually walk through the front entrance of her station. Maybe even worse.

"Not now, Miss Rosa. We are very busy today, as you can probably -"

"I know who killed my sister, Veena." By the look on her face I'd say she only fifty percent believed that I had someone in mind. Not that I had the right person, but that I just had someone in general.

"And what have you gone through to obtain such evidence that I'm guessing you are wishing to present to me?"

"It doesn't matter what I went through, and yes of course I have evidence."

"And why should I believe that a fourteen-year-old girl didn't somehow stretch the truth while meddling in my case?" The fact that she cared more about procedures and technicalities than uncovering the truth in an unlawful manslaughter was mind boggling, but I guess that was just business for you in the universe of many police officers.

"First of all, I'm sixteen, and second, it's not your case, it's Detective Baron's. And he's done more work on this case than you realize. Now, where are officers Rickers and Smith?"

"Why do you want to know where they are?"

Something seemed off. The tightness in her brow suggested she genuinely had no idea why I would need to speak with them. After all, they weren't assigned to the case, and they were just low-level cops.

"Nova!" Tom called out to me from down the hall. "I've got it. I've got the tapes. We were right. The time of Veena's accident, it's nothing but sand. I've got a copy of them right here." He held up a flash drive as he caught his breath.

"Can someone please explain to me what's going on here?" Sanders cried out. Turns out she had more prominent, echoing pipes than I thought.

"Ma'am," Tom spoke up with confidence and no hesitation. "We have reason to believe Officers Rickers and Smith were the ones that hit Veena Rosa and left her there to die."

Sanders wasn't angry. Believe me, I already learned what an angry Sanders looked like. She didn't talk. She didn't flinch. She didn't even blink for a few seconds before she turned to a random officer in the hallway and said, "Officer Hobb, can you please get Rickers and Smith over here? I need to speak with them."

I wouldn't have blamed Tom if he wanted to crack a little smile for feeling accomplished for just a brief moment, but it wasn't a celebration for him. He took no pride in accusing his coworkers and dealing with criminals. It wasn't an achievement for him, because he wasn't doing this for them, or himself, not even for the community or me. He was doing this for Veena.

"Yes, Captain?" said Rickers as he stepped forward with his hands on his belt. I don't know what happened to me there, but it was almost as if I could read his mind. What his mind was telling me, was that he knew exactly why Sanders had retrieved him. He was nervous, but not ashamed. My guess is that he hadn't lost an ounce of sleep over this.

Smith on the other hand, his forehead crinkled in one straight line from temple to temple. He heavily lacked confidence, but it was almost as if he was trying to copy Rickers. His thumbs tucked behind his belt just like Rickers' did, but Smith's eyes bounced back and forth from Sanders and Rickers like a yoyo.

"Where were you two on the night of the Rosa hit and run?" Sanders asked.

"Oh, Ma'am we already told you this, remember?" Rickers began to mansplain. "We were involved in a car chase that led us away from our original post. It was a 2001 Chevy, and I'm sure we have the license plate number somewhere. It unfortunately got away." He smiled as though he was just so satisfied with the "lesson" he just gave her. Of course, he was a cop after all.

"Really?" said Sanders. I had never heard her voice so calm and tame. She was in total control. "Did you know I tracked that vehicle down? It had some issues. I received a report from a mechanic and apparently its acceleration and engine were rather weak. Let me ask you this..." Her smile almost mocked Rickers' which, of course, made his slide right off. "How did it get away if the vehicle was barely even drivable? You could have easily caught that. Unless something interrupted you?"

There was nothing more that I wanted than to present myself as bullet proof right then and there. For Veena, and for myself, but my bullet-proof vest seemed to already have some holes in it. My head vigorously shook back and forth, and my fingertips clenched into my palm. The more I learned about how my sister was taken away from me, the more overwhelming the whole case felt. Jack put his hand on my back and almost had to keep me from falling over.

"That might have been a mistake, Captain. I do not believe that was the case." He wasn't giving in. Smith thought he was helping by standing there nodding with the corners of his mouth drooping to his chin. Who were these guys?

"I don't believe so. Detective Baron, would you mind presenting to me the evidence you have that supports these officer's involvement in the Rosa case?"

"Of course, Ma'am." There was no, *I would love to.* There was no, *Gladly.* Just, *Of course, Ma'am.* "Here we have their body camera recordings which have partially been erased from that day."

Maybe I was mistaken from all my emotions having a dance party in my chest and head, but I could have sworn I saw a smile of satisfaction creep upon her face for just one moment. Or even just a fraction of a moment. For some reason, I felt like there was probably more to that smile than I knew.

"Also, Ma'am," said Tom. "Their cruiser, 641, has had a repainting recently that was not reported and whoever touched it up, did so poorly. Therefore, it was probably not done by a professional."

"I see." This was the exact moment when the two officers knew they were absolutely screwed, but Rickers looked more inconvenienced than anything. There didn't seem to be any remorse present. No guilt, but what was really pulling my attention away from everything else was why Sanders hadn't read them their rights and arrested them yet.

"I'm just wondering," she began once again. "How did they get their hands on the paint to retouch the cruiser? I'd be surprised if either one of them knew where it would be."

She had a bit of a point, I guess, but why couldn't these questions wait until later? Unless she was suggesting -

"Ma'am?" Rickers asked. "Is all of this really necessary? You don't actually believe this do you? Like you pointed out, there are a lot of flaws in this...well...theory." Jack was standing about a foot away from me, but I could still feel the steam swirling off his skin. Anyone could feel his anger in the room, which was a feeling he didn't emote often.

Like usual, Sanders kept her composure. She held up Tom's flash drive and gave it a little shake, almost bragging to him. "I'm going to have myself a look at this. Would you gentlemen like to join me?" It was an amusing moment, but I couldn't laugh. I couldn't even smile. Naturally, my almost amused eyes stared them down, and I could still see the fear plastered from Smith's eyebrows to his knees.

"Wait," Smith gently shouted. Rickers completely pivoted his feet and looked like he was about to throw Smith into the ceiling.

"Yes, Officer Smith?" Sanders asked, pushing for more. But he had no words. What could Rickers possibly be threatening him with besides physical abuse? "Yes?"

"Ma'am," Rickers cut Smith off before he could say anything. "We did nothing wrong. Miss Rosa ran into us. We were afraid this was an act of aggression and protest. We also considered maybe it was an attempted suicide."

I had seen a few movies and T.V. shows where the parents of a victim were offended when law enforcement would suggest that their child committed suicide or they asked if they were suicidal. I never understood why that was such a big deal, until now.

"That's a goddamn lie," I snapped with no regret. "I read my sister's diary. I was with her almost twenty-four-seven. I spied on her and her friends. She was in no way suicidal. And she certainly wasn't stupid enough to protest like that. She had her opinions, but she expressed them honorably. WHAT KIND OF COP ARE YOU?"

It was just now that I realized I had been slowly walking toward this coward as I was speaking. I'd love to say he felt even a touch of intimidation, but he just stood his ground and kept all six-foot-four of him planted and still.

"I'm a cop," he almost whispered in a threatening manner. "That should be enough for you."

"You're sick, you know that?" I whispered back to him, but he only responded with a small huff and a pop in the corner of his mouth. His eyes didn't break away from mine, but I could tell that they wanted to.

"Officer Smith," Sanders tried once more. "I really would like to hear what you have to say."

Smith was an inch away from cracking. Then it was more like a centimeter, and then...

"Rickers just turned so fast. He said that he didn't need to follow the speed limit when no one was around because he's a cop. After we hit her, he told me that even cops have secrets, and he said my career would be over if I ever told anybody."

Instead of throwing Smith across the room like I assumed he would, Rickers closed his eyes, saw his future flash before him, and reopened them to watch his career come to a sharp end.

Sanders pointed to two other officers and said, "Danvers and Howard, take Rickers to interrogation room seven and Smith to eight."

"Wait!" I said, catching Smith's attention before they could leave. "Officer, I need to ask you something." His frightened face gave me no response, but he knew what I was about to ask. "Did you know that my sister was still alive when you left her?" Again, no response, but that was all I needed. He stood there with empty eyes and an empty soul. "No." My lip quivered so harshly that I just kept mumbling "No." I wasn't sure what else I could say. If Veena was hit by anybody else, she might still be here.

I almost plunged into him. Just to see if it would make me feel any better to force even an ounce of pain into him. But before I could do anything, Jack sensed what I was thinking, rushed up to me, and grabbed a hold of me before I could collapse. One of his sweaty hands held onto mine while the other wrapped around my waist. His head fell close to mine as I could feel his tears dripping down almost as fast as my own.

"Officers Smith and Rickers," Sanders began, taking out her handcuffs, with Tom following. "You are both under arrest for the manslaughter of Veena Rosa. You are also both relieved of your duties as law enforcement officers of the United States. You have the right to remain silent..." She read them the rest of their rights and reminded them how much of a disgrace they were. "I wish you two knew how much you don't deserve to wear these badges, but you never will." I don't know why, but I think these were the words that I was going to remember the most. When I thought of this day, this was the moment I was going to replay in my mind over and over again. I was afraid it would never end.

"What is going on over here?!" I heard the Lieutenant yell at the top of his lungs.

"Lieutenant Barry, these now civilians are under arrest. I can handle this, please." There was a bit more mumbling going on, but I couldn't hear everything over my difficulty in breathing.

"What have they told you? I'm sure this is all just a misunderstanding. They couldn't have hurt anyone. These are some of my best guys." From my crouching position, I looked up at this man's face and through my watery eyes, I could have sworn I saw this man smile. Did he think this was funny? What could be so amusing to him? And who even was this guy?

"These men are under arrest," Tom fiercely chimed in. "In case you didn't hear her. If you have a problem with it, present a testimony in court."

Tom clamped the handcuffs so tight on Smith's wrist, the poor sucker flinched, but only a little bit. And the crazy part was, I did too. I was still trying to figure out why, but before I could think more about it, Tom brought a pensive look upon his face as he started to walk the men to their holding cells with the two other officers.

"Sir," he stopped in his tracks, speaking to the Lieutenant. "Did you claim they didn't hurt anyone just now?"

"Yes, of course they didn't. That's the truth."

"How did you know that they hurt someone? You just chimed into the conversation and we just proposed our theory about them to Sanders not even five minutes ago." The heavy man started to sweat more than Smith.

"I just assumed. That's usually what we arrest people for."

"Really? How did you know they didn't steal something? Or commit obstruction of justice. I think your story is a little flawed, Lieutenant." Tom's face was even closer than mine was to Rickers'. "I was wondering earlier how they got access to destroying the tapes from when they hit Miss Rosa. They couldn't get access to it. Or where they got the cruiser paint from. So, it had to be someone of a higher ranking. Perhaps a lieutenant?" There it was, that laughter was back. That stupid, disgusting, conceited laughter.

"This is ridiculous. Why would I do such a thing? You have no proof!" Tom threw his hands in the air in what was probably a mixture of both anger and astonishment.

"Ah. The three things you should never say when you are being interrogated by a detective."

"But you're not much of a detective, are you, Baron?" The satisfaction in this man's eyes for asking such a question. He couldn't be prouder of himself. It was scary to learn and think about how many dirty cops there were in this town.

"I'm not the one being accused of accessory to manslaughter."

"Like I said," Barry crossed his arms as if he were a toddler not getting his juice box. "Prove it."

Tom took a moment to drop his head and think. It was fine. I didn't worry. He would find something. But man, I was getting impatient.

Think, Tom, think. We can't let this guy go.

"Tom," said Sanders, using his first name for probably the first time. "Why would he be involved?"

"Rickers' recruitment." It was like a lightbulb for Tom. A bright, sixty-watt light bulb that snapped on right above his head. "Didn't they originally come from the same precinct in New York? Barry vouched for him, remember? Rickers must have come to him for help, and when he did, Barry couldn't refuse because he was the one that brought Rickers here. He was afraid he would be penalized for bringing such a dirty cop to the station."

This made me look at the lieutenant the same way I looked at Rickers. I tried not to at all, but I couldn't help it. If this man hadn't brought Rickers here, Veena would still be alive. My sister would still be here with me. That stupid butterfly effect...it changed everything for me.

"You still need to give me some proof, detective," Barry snapped.

"I'm getting to that, if only you would have some patience like a real detective." I was still crouched on the floor, feeling too low and shivery to stand up, but this was what made me perk up and fight to give my full attention through my tears. "The key card. They keep records of everyone who passes through, and how long they stay in there. If he went in some time shortly after the accident that'll be enough for an arrest. People don't go in there that often."

The energy everyone else carried suggested this was a solid plan, until Barry shook it off with a smile and an almost misogynistic shake of the head.

"No," Tom continued. "You already deleted that."

"I'm not saying nothing," Barry responded like the true criminal that he was.

"Well, let me just ask you this simple question and I'll read from your eyes if it's true or not. Does that sound good?" He cleared his throat and made even firmer eye contact with Barry than before. "Did you erase those digital records before or after Sunday morning? Because in case you didn't know, we copy those records, including many others throughout this station every Sunday morning on a hard drive."

Barry's ears and the corners of his mouth shot to the back of his head. But the anger in his eyes grew to the point that they looked like they were about to burst into flames. It was almost as if he was allergic to embarrassment and vulnerability. I hoped to never understand what that was like.

"We'll check that later," said Sanders. "We have our answer. Detective Baron, would you do the honors?"

Tom snapped the cuffs on him, but still, he didn't seem to feel honorable about it. It looked like he was about to start doing dishes. The worst part of the day, and this was the worst part about his job.

The real detective read Former Lieutenant Barry his rights and brought all three of the handcuffed men down the hall, but I didn't notice exactly where they went. I was still too busy having trouble breathing, and Jack still had his hand on my back. He had never left my side.

"Just breathe, okay?" Jack reminded me. "Is your chest okay? Or does it feel tight? We might need to lay you down."

I nodded my head since I was unintentionally clutching onto my chest with both of my fists. He brought me over to the closest bench that might have been about twenty feet away from the double glass doors. And just like Veena's funeral, I got pissed at the goddamn sun once again. It was too bright, and all I wanted to do was numb myself. I didn't want to feel. If I felt anything at all, it was going to be pain. I only wanted to fall asleep, and it wouldn't have been the worst thing in the world if I stayed asleep for a while. At least that's just what was going through my head.

"Is this better?" Jack asked after he laid my head on his lap.

"Yeah," I managed to squeeze the words out of my mouth. I was probably about to drench his jean shorts.

"It's okay." He gently shook my shoulder. "It's all over. They've got them. They're going to prison and pay for what they did. I promise you they *will* be convicted."

"That - that's the thing," I said after the biggest gasp of air.

"What do you mean?"

"It's over. This wasn't a happy ending. It was all just screwed up, and she's still gone. She's not coming back. She might exist in this other world, but that's not my world. It's not real. I don't know what it is, but it's not real. Even if it was, I have to leave that world behind now that it's over. I can't keep coming back into a world where my sister doesn't exist. It's just not right. I can't grieve and move on like that. I really didn't want this to be the answer. I really wish I could stay in a place where my sister is forever and ever, but I can't. It's not mine, and my parents need me."

Jack didn't know what to say, but he didn't need to say anything. Like always, he knew what I needed and what to do. I didn't know what magic he possessed, but I was grateful he had it.

"Nova," Sanders gently called me as she walked over and crouched down next to me. "Nova, I'm so sorry. I don't know what we would have done without you, but you did it. They're going to pay for what happened."

I knew saying that I had suspected her before all of this would definitely be the wrong choice, but it did cross my mind. Mainly because I couldn't believe how grateful I was for her. She finally believed me. It took a while, but I didn't care anymore. It sounded weird and maybe a little cliché, but I think Veena's voice was in my head saying that I needed to forgive her for her mistakes. And as much as it pained me to think about it, I think she was also saying that I needed to forgive the men involved in her death. That's exactly what she would have done. I knew that to be true. She would still be leading the way for me like the big sister she still was even though she was gone. I would never stop learning from her.

"Captain," said Jack, "Would someone be able to give us a ride home?"

"Of course. I'll bring you home myself."

PART 12: AUGUST 9TH, 5:04PM

Jack said he would come with me for my last trip to the other world, but I kept putting it off. On Monday, I said, "Let's go tomorrow," but I lied and told him I didn't feel well. He knew I was lying before I even said anything, but he didn't put an ounce of pressure on me. He knew I needed to be in the right headspace to do this, and he trusted it was gonna happen eventually, I just needed a little bit of time.

Finally, on Friday, I felt that the time was right. Not because I was prepared. I knew that was never gonna happen, but because I felt peaceful for some reason. Maybe it was because I finally decided to forgive the goddamn sun for everything that it had done the past couple of weeks, but that's still undecided.

Jack came over at around eleven in the morning, so I wouldn't feel anxious, waiting around for most of the day. And in classic Jack fashion, he came with a gift.

"I got something for you," he said, holding up a plastic bag.

"Such beautiful wrapping," I joked.

"Okay, I will admit, I just came up with this idea like twenty minutes ago. So, I ran to the store and got what they had."

Like I said, gifts were a classic Jack behavior, and so was procrastination. How that boy got straight As was beyond me.

"Thank you," I laughed, taking the bag from him. I frantically opened it like I always open gifts. Before me were two brand new mugs that both said, "Always". Me and Veena's favorite Harry Potter quote, or whatever you would call that one-word sentence. One tear ran down my cheek, but it wasn't a sad tear. This was a tear that reminded me of what I still had in my life. "You know, I told myself a few months ago that I was gonna have a great summer with my sister...and you of course, but mainly Veena." Jack chuckled enough to show off his laugh lines. "Instead, I got to have a terrible one with her. But I'm so unbelievably grateful that I got to have at least that. I think that's what this bridge was truly for at the end of the day. Not just to help me solve her case. Not just so I could see her again, but to show me that I have the ability and strength to realize that I'm still so lucky for everything I still have. Some person or thing out there knew I was going to seriously doubt that, and - I guess they sent me help. I survived losing her over and over again, or at least that's what it felt like, and I know that I have to do it one more time, but this time I know that I can do it."

Jack took my hand and said, "Of course you can. Veena always had confidence in you. And...you know I'm not religious or anything. Neither of us are, but I bet you she still does."

I have to admit, I agreed with him. I could just feel it. Maybe that would go away, but I was okay with not knowing what the future held for me.

"I'm ready," I said, staring at the bridge right in front of me.

"I don't care how long it takes, okay? You can be in there for days if you need to be. I'm going to be here right when you get back. I'm not going anywhere." Jack was a pretty serious person, but I don't think he had been more serious about anything in his entire life.

"I'm not going to be in there for days," I giggled. "I just need to say my goodbyes. That's really it."

"I love you, you know that?" Being best friends, we said that to each other almost every day, but the way he said it was different. He said it because I needed to hear it and because he needed to say it. Not just because it was our usual formality.

"I love you so much. I don't know what I would do without you." In my opinion, reminding people how much you need them is sometimes more necessary than saying that you love them. Not necessarily more important, it can just say more, *and* remind people *why* you love them so much. I wish I had said that to Veena more often, but she knew. Thank God I had such a smart and understanding person as my sister. Otherwise, I would have been screwed for so many reasons.

"I'll be right back."

"Handshake?" He held out his hand in front of him with eyebrows lifted and only a little crack in his smile.

"Always." And after two pats on the palm, a slide down each other's forearms, and the least sassy snaps in the history of finger snapping, I walked into the other world for the last time.

I didn't rush to look for her. I had no desire to be out of breath any time soon. I'd had enough of that crap. I checked her workplace, I checked my mom's house. The only two other places she could be was at Raya's or my dad's. Obviously, I was checking my dad's first.

Just like I wanted it to be, the day was a dreary one. No rain yet, but it was definitely coming. Finally, some appropriate weather for the day. Somehow, it relaxed me, but only my body. Not so much my mind.

Good ole Dad stood at the island in the kitchen that had a minimum of seventeen cracks and chips in it. The smell of baked potatoes and green beans shot up my nose almost the moment I stepped in. Something was also probably burning because it was John Rosa's cooking, but I hadn't noticed anything yet.

"Hey, Dad," I said so I wouldn't scare him.

"Oh hey, kiddo. You lookin' for your sister?" Man, this world worked wonders.

"It's like you read my mind." I tried to force a smile, so he couldn't *actually* read my mind, but I think it came out all twitchy and weird.

"Everythin' alright?"

I shook my head as I bit my lip. "No, but it will be." I rarely lied to my dad. I wasn't sure why since I was a sixteen-year-old girl that snuck out of her mother's house every other night, but it was the kind of connection that we had that made me feel like there was no reason to hide anything.

"Always will be, kiddo."

We ate some dinner while we waited for her. Apparently, she *was* at Raya's, working on their summer reading, and believe me, you don't wanna be near Raya when she's doing school work. Either she will be extra snippy, or you'll feel your brain melt from listening to her attempt to read or do math.

Along with stuffing our faces, we exchanged stories from our week and a few from our distant pasts. By that, I mean my dad mainly reminded me of stories from when I forgot the words in my fourth-grade musical production of *Annie* when I, of course, played the tiniest character, Molly. But I told him about the vision boards that Jack and I were going to make...and that was mainly it. Spending good, quality time with my dad was rare. Which honestly, was stupid. He didn't live that far away. But losing Veena reminded me that I couldn't wait for, or gamble with these things. John Rosa was an amazing dad. He deserved all the time in the world, and now it was my job to constantly remind him of that.

"Hey, Dad," Veena quietly yelled when she swung the front door open. I could hear her high-heeled sneakers run through the hallway and into the kitchen. "Oh hey, you. Didn't expect to see you here. Thought you'd be at Mom's tonight."

"Yeah, well -" My voice started cracking, and a lump in my throat was creeping up. Dammit. Now was not the time to cry. Not yet anyway.

"Why don't you two go for a walk tonight?" Dad suggested after noticing my struggle. "Seems like some sister and girl time is needed, or whatever it is you kids call it these days."

"Sounds like a plan to me," said Veena. "You down?"

My glossy eyes smiled along with the rest of my face as I nodded and got up from my chair.

The moment we stepped out of the house, we began the slowest walk of all time. Mainly because I never wanted it to end, but I also rarely felt this much stiffness in my body.

"Hey," Veena gently snapped. "What's wrong?"

I stopped walking and turned to face her with as much confidence as I could. "Veena, so many things are wrong right now that shouldn't have happened. But...they did. Now I have to learn to accept that."

The weirdest thing happened after that. She looked at me as if she...*understood*. I'd lost count as to how many times I'd been in this world, but it still amazed and confused me at the same time.

"What do you need me to do?" Veena asked.

She looked at me like she had always looked at me. She smiled at me knowing she was going to see me again. And you know, what? I believed her.

"Nothing," I sighed, still shivering. "I don't need you to do anything. I came here thinking I was going to make this whole speech. But that's just not necessary. What else is there to say? You're an amazing sister, you know that?"

"Of course, I do. Duh." We both laughed like we always did. She never failed to make me laugh. "Are you sure there isn't anything you want to tell me?"

I thought about that question long and hard for a moment, because the truth was...well, no. Everything that I needed to tell her I already had. Every important moment that I had in my life, she had either experienced with me, or I'd laid out in explicit detail for her. But it wasn't really about those times anyway. She knew how much I needed her, always. She sure as hell wasn't ever gonna forget that. If I ever felt like I needed to remind her, I knew exactly where to find her, and I knew she would hear me.

"You already know everything I've ever needed to tell you. What I really want to do right now is just hug you, okay? Because I'm not sure when that's going to happen again. It might be a while."

"But why -?" Veena started to say.

"Shhh!" That was all I needed to say to stop her questions.

Silently, she hugged me almost as tight as I hugged her. Somehow, she knew why I began to cry. I mean, she might not have truly known, but she knew that she needed to cry too. I never wanted to let go, but I knew this moment was the most important moment for my grieving. I was so lucky to have this, and that just made me cry even more.

It could have been ten minutes. It could have been an hour. I'm still not sure, but we stayed silent the whole time. Finally, I broke the silence by wiping my face and saying, "Will you do something for me?" She smiled and nodded before we stood up and walked to the bridge.

The entire walk there, I squeezed her hand. Occasionally I would look over to her and admire her smile. We had similar smiles. Both of us got them from our beautiful mother. All three of us had plump lips with laugh lines and dimples. That was probably the only thing Veena and I had in common now that I thought of it.

I swear, on that short walk over, I went through our entire lives together. Like the time Veena dared me to pee behind the snowman we made when I was seven, and I did, or the time she jumped on my bed after her first date when she was fourteen and told me all about her amazing first kiss with some guy named Casey. I didn't care if I had to go to meditation therapy to remember every single memory that we had together. I would never allow a single second to disappear from my mind.

And before I knew it, we arrived at the bridge. I thought that facing her killer would be the hardest part, or hearing the news about her death would be the hardest part. But this was the most grueling moment in my journey of grief so far. I mean, I feel like that would be a given, but it was such an odd moment. This was the deepest daze I had ever spiraled into in my entire life. Nothing seemed real, and for all I knew, it might not have been, but this was also the place that I wanted to be the most in the entire world. I would never want to be robbed of the chance of saying goodbye to my big sister. I wish everybody had the chance that I did.

Veena took a second to admire the bridge. Her smile didn't leave her face for a second as she reminisced about the times she spent sitting on that bridge listening to me whine and complain about anything and everything. Why was she smiling? Well...because she was Veena.

"My favorite memory of you on this bridge was when you and Jack had your first friendship fight."

"Really?" I asked, wiping my face. "I don't remember that."

"He asked you for a piece of your Halloween candy and you said no. Do you know what kind of candy he asked for?"

"Which kind?"

"Snickers."

If I had any kind of liquid in my mouth it would have shot out of my nose from laughter. "But I hate Snickers."

"I know. That's how much of a brat you were!"

I rested my head on her shoulder as we continued to giggle our little heads off. It barely reached since she was almost a full head taller than me, but I always thought it was cute and funny.

"Promise me something?" I asked my sister.

"Anything."

"The next time I see you, we will be laughing just like this. Uncontrollable and high pitched. It will be like we never left each other."

She looked at me as if she knew exactly what had happened in my world. Maybe she did, but she at least knew that we would be apart for quite some time.

"I couldn't imagine it any other way."

I wanted to give her one last hug. The biggest and tightest one I had ever given her, but I wanted to take one last look first. Her pure happiness. Her health. Everything the way it should have been. That's how I wanted to remember her.

"I'm going to hug you now, but it can only last about ten seconds, okay? Because if it goes for any longer I don't know if I'll be able to let go, alright?"

She smiled with her glossy eyes and gave me one little nod before she wrapped her long skinny arms around me as if she would never be able to embrace another human being again. I began to count down, and Veena followed along with me.

"Ten."

"Nine."

"Eight."

"Seven."

"Six."

"Five."

"Four."

"Three."

"Two."

"One."

And somehow...I let go. I extended my arm out as I backed up, and her fingers slipped through mine. The last time I saw my sister's face, she was okay. She was at peace. I'd like to think she still was. In my own world that is. I didn't stop looking at her bright smile as I stepped backwards under the bridge.

"I love you so much, Nova," Veena whispered.

"I love you too, Veena," I whispered back, one last time, as her image began to disintegrate, and I was back in my own world.

"Nova!" I heard Jack holler right behind me as I collapsed backwards into his arms, but I was safe. Everything was still fuzzy, but I survived. Somehow, I felt weak and strong at the same time. "Are you okay?"

"No," I croaked. "But I did it, so I will be. I said goodbye to her....I did it."

"I'm so proud of you." Jack always reminded me how great of a hugger he was whenever he hugged me. His chin dug so deep into my shoulder I almost had to tell him to lighten up, but I didn't. I needed his comfort more than anything. "You are the strongest person I know. Do you know that?" Even after he told me that, I still didn't believe him, but maybe in time I would. I hoped I would at least. It was always Veena and Jack that reminded me how awesome of a human being I was. Veena was still reminding me to this day.

"You really think so?" I asked him.

"I know so." We stayed there for a few more minutes, wiping away our tears, and trying to think about what on Earth to do next.

"I'm scared I'll be tempted to go back there. I know I will in the future at least. I'm not even sure if I can. Now that I got what I needed, I might not be able to, but I really don't want to know."

Jack rubbed my shoulder, gently picked me up off the dirty ground and said, "We should probably go back home then. Is that okay?" I slowly smiled and nodded, almost not wanting to. "Also I have an idea."

A few days later, Jack came up with the perfect plan. Since the old bridge was about to snap any day now, we got some money to rebuild it. Not that it cost that much anyways. It was about as big as I was after all, but we wanted the new one to be fancy. Just as Veena would have liked. Also, it turned out Tom was handy with a hammer.

"Remind me why we have to tear this bridge down?" Tom asked, pushing a pile of wood on a dolly and into the woods. "It sounds like it's really important to you, Nova."

"It is," I replied, struggling to carry a bucket of tools even though it looked like there was only a hammer, nails, screws, and a screw gun in it. "But I want this spot to be a place for kids, or even adults to go to if they wanna. I don't want it to break down or anything. Everything needs an update eventually. Besides, I wanna do something special with it. You'll see."

Unloading my dad's truck was the easy part, but getting the supplies down the pathway and to the bridge was a whole different story. Tom kept stopping for breaks and asking, "Are you sure you don't want any of your family members to help?" But I wanted it to be a surprise for them, and Jack was actually a lot stronger than he looked. Those modified push-ups were paying off.

When we flopped all of the supplies in front of the bridge and immediately started chugging our waters, Tom nervously looked at his shoes and said, "Hey, I'm sorry I didn't get a chance to apologize to you about everything that happened. And I'm sorry that you had to do all of the work you did. It wasn't supposed to be your job. I can't imagine what was going through your head."

"So, you're sorry about being sorry about being sorry?" After my snarky comment, I realized Tom *still* hadn't been around me enough to understand how humor helped me cope with...well pretty much everything. Luckily, he caught on.

"When you put it that way, yes? I think?" In a weird way, he kind of reminded me of my sister. They both listened to me when most people didn't. They were both way more capable of success than they thought they were, but they also never took anyone's crap.

"I hope you know I wouldn't have been able to do any of this without you. Thank you for listening. You're an amazing cop, and I will probably never say that about another cop ever again."

"Thank you, Nova. I appreciate that."

"I'm going to forgive them, you know." I was half expecting Tom to freak out or call me crazy, but he just stood there and continued to listen. "Not anytime soon, but I wanna forgive them. I don't know why, but I do. I feel like I have to, like it will be the final stage of closure and moving on. I think that'll be really beautiful."

"I think that will be an amazing feeling."

I nodded my head and bit my cheek before I said, "I'm sorry you had to work with such dirty cops. I don't know if my suspicions are correct, but that must feel like you've been betrayed in some way. Cops are supposed to protect us, not hurt us in any way shape or form."

"I can't promise perfection, Nova, but I want to protect these streets, and I will make damn certain that not a single dirty cop will ever walk through those doors ever again."

I didn't mean to look like a douche by chuckling a little bit, but his confidence was quite extreme. "You, yourself will make sure of that?"

"Well," he said as if he had the best news to give. I had yet to see him excited about anything. "Captain Sanders promoted me to Lieutenant."

"What?" I screamed out, "I mean, Lieutenant is a good thing, right?"

"It's a raise and a new car, so yes." I gave him such an intense high five, I had to shake out my hand.

"What are we celebrating?" Jack asked, walking down the ditch and carrying more wood.

"Detective Baron here is now a Lieutenant, whatever that means, since the old one was a lying old dirt bag." Not my best diss, but it was something.

"Hot damn, Lieutenant. Nice! Drinks for celebration?"

"Nice try," Tom replied, shaking his head. "Come on, let's get to work."

Taking down the old bridge was surprisingly quick and easy. Turns out I was right. It probably *was* about to snap in half. But it had lived a good, sturdy, long life. Thankfully for me, it wasn't nearly as gut-wrenching as I thought it was gonna be. It was sort of like taking down your childhood swing set; sad, but the memories would last and there was still so much to look forward to. So many more memories to make in the yard. A new beginning.

It took us about eight hours to finish the new one. It would have been seven if Jack hadn't insisted on ordering Wendy's for lunch which was in the next town over, but every moment was worth it. We listened to banging oldie music like Elton John and Elvis. Two of Veena's favorites.

For most of the time, Tom put me in charge of gluing and Jack in charge of screwing with the gun. That mainly left Tom in charge of cutting the wood with the portable jigsaw since Jack and I were both too scared to use it but not too scared to admit it. After an hour of digging the ends of the bridge into the rocks and dirt, it came time to put on the first part of the finishing touch; the railings. The old one didn't have anything of the sort, but I wanted to make sure there was room for any small child to sit on the edge and kick their feet as madly as they wanted.

Tom was particularly creative when it came to bending the slim pieces of wood to create exquisite flipped curves at the ends, and I don't use the word, "exquisite" to describe just anything.

And for the second part of the finishing touch, I had no idea how to go about it.

"Lieutenant," I said, catching Tom's attention. He was getting the hang of this lieutenant business. "If I wanted to permanently write something along the bridge - like carve it - What would I use?"

Tom pondered for a moment before he pulled out, yet again, another tool that I really didn't want to use, or at least it looked that way.

"What about this cylindrical bit? You clip it into the tip of the screw gun and you can basically just draw with it."

My wide eyes didn't even blink as Tom put the gun in my hand. "Um, okay. Actually, maybe Jack should do it."

"Shut up and screw, you wuss!" Jack hollered to me as he threw a candy wrapper in my face. Generation Z has weird ways of boosting their friend's confidence. Even Millennial Tom laughed with us as they helped me up on the ladder and I started slicing the wood away. Carving the words was surprisingly a lot easier than I thought. Of course, the hardest letter was the letter "G", but the next hardest letter was actually "V". I guess my confidence grew too quickly. Either that or I was just that uncoordinated, but I'll go with the first one.

Finally, right before the sky turned into a beautiful nightfall, the bridge was finished. I thanked Tom for helping us on his only day off and told him to be free, but he didn't wanna miss the look on my parents' faces. Neither did Jack.

I could have waited for daylight the next day, but what fun would that be? And my impatience was killing me. I texted all three of my parents to meet me at the spot where I would always enter the woods; between the two biggest trees in the forest. I was beyond elated that they remembered where it was.

The three of us each took a parent to cover their eyes and walk them down to the bridge. Mom was miserable and cranky. She thought it was a prank because it usually was, but I had a feeling that would just make her happier to see what we did.

We stood them in a perfect line in the ditch as we all counted down; "THREE, TWO, ONE!"

And just like that, all three of their jaws dropped as they read "THE VEENA ROSA BRIDGE" written across the newly renovated, freshly made bridge.

Just like I predicted, my mom crouched down to her feet, like I did in the station, but she couldn't take her eyes off it. The design was mediocre at best, but to her it was the most beautiful thing she'd ever seen. The three of them embraced each other just like they did at the funeral before they walked over to get a better look at our work and touch one of their newest beloved possessions.

For the first time in over a month, I felt a little bit of peace. Not a ton, but a small droplet. And it was the first time I believed it when I told myself that I was going to be truly happy again one day. Somehow, I would be okay.

We all must have stayed there for an hour. We took some pictures, told some stories. It all just made me more excited to show everyone else. Everyone was gonna love it whether they liked it or not.

PART 13: FEBRUARY 15TH, 11:17AM

February 15th 2020. Veena's eighteenth birthday, and our first birthday without her. Honestly, I was a bit lost. Veena hated her birthday, and my only guess as to why was because, regardless of what people thought about her, she despised overexaggerated attention. Still, it's not like we had much of a choice. We had to do something. She wasn't physically here on this earth anymore, and the only way to keep her around was to celebrate her.

The cemetery was a lot brighter than usual. I'd been there a few times to visit her in the past few months, but it was hard. I also hadn't been there with my mom yet. She had only been there before two other times; when the headstone was finished and on Christmas. My mom brought Veena what she probably would have wanted for Christmas; a new pink necklace with a flower on it, and purple mittens.

For my birthday gift, I brought Veena her favorite meal from Bernie's; blueberry pancakes with maple syrup from New Hampshire. Lauren almost cried when I asked her to make it for Veena. She probably did when making it behind the counter. Then she asked me if I was going to end up eating it, and I of course said yes. She laughed as she passed me the pancakes with a sweet little note and refused to take my debit card when I tried to pay her.

The note said, "Happy eighteenth, beautiful girl. I hope you're eating pancakes wherever you are." With the tearful words she drew hearts all over the card. I already had a frame ready for it at home.

Just like we predicted, we were the only ones at the cemetery. Everything was peaceful, even with the sadness and sorrow in the air. I couldn't believe how proud I was of my mom for not crying. Even though it would have been more than okay if she did, but she held it together. She missed her baby girl, but she felt Veena's presence just as much as I did.

"Hey look!" I said to my mother as we set up the lawn chairs next to Veena's grave. I pulled up a picture of the newest addition to the bridge. For the past couple of months, people from all over town had been leaving presents and flowers at our newly renovated bridge. Some people had even glued or painted pictures of her on the wood itself. Of course, I often visited, and I would always show my parents a picture when someone brought something new. This time it was a teddy bear with a giant "V" on its belly. It kind of looked like a heart and was probably supposed to be for Valentine's day, but we loved it anyway.

"Oh, isn't that precious," my mom said, putting her hand over her heart, and pouting her lips. Those were the exact words she used every time somebody put a new gift on the bridge. Except for the time an old childhood friend of Veena's put a framed picture of them at their birthday party when they were probably seven. They were all super cute huddled in their swimsuits and eating pizza. I couldn't remember what his name was, but my mother wouldn't stop shaking and crying. She insisted on making a copy and putting it in her new picture book specifically for Veena.

"Hey everyone!" My dad said as he pulled up in his truck with a basketful of balloons and flowers. "Sorry I'm a little late." He was always late. That was basically his catch phrase.

My parents, Ralph, and I all sat beside Veena's grave under our blankets. We didn't stay for too long, but it was long enough that occasionally we would have to rip our gloves off and breathe on our hands as we tried to make a fire with them.

Right as we were about to leave, Jack popped up in his new minivan that he paid for himself (and wouldn't let me forget it) right after he got his license a few months before.

"Hi," he gently greeted us. "Is it okay if I crash?" He held his hands behind his back which usually meant he was overly excited to tell me something and was growing impatient.

"Of course, Jack," my mom told him. "But we were just about to leave."

"That's okay. Sorry I just..." Jack didn't usually get too flustered, but he seemed more overwhelmed than usual.

"Dork, spit it out!" I joked.

"Hold your horses!" He released one arm behind him to give me the, *calm down, Nova* hand. "Someone just put a new present on the bridge."

"Who?" My dad asked.

Jack held his chest up, prouder of himself than he'd been in a long time, and said, "Captain Sanders, Lieutenant Baron, and me."

To be real, my mom looked scared. Jack seemed pumped, but he wasn't always the best with gifts. One year he gave me an ant farm when we were ten, and it broke under my mom's new sofa. She was maaaaaad.

"Thank you, Jack. That's really sweet of you," said Ralph through gritted and nervous teeth. He was actually the one that had paid for that sofa. "What is it?"

"You're going to have to come and see. It's too awesome."

Don't get me wrong. I was really eager to see what he got, even if it was weird, but I was really cold and those pancakes were really getting to me, so I said, "Okay, let's get there quick then!"

Mom and I said, "Happy birthday" to Veena's grave, and we all headed over to the bridge. Jack insisted that I ride with him and listen to his new stereo system.

Mom was probably the least happy to have to walk through the single inch of snow in the woods. She grew up in Southern California, so I guess I understood. Jack kept on rubbing his hands together in excitement and didn't let the giant grin fall from his face. Ralph and Dad had to keep helping each other up when they slipped and fell on icy patches. They were both klutzes, so I guess Mom had a type. Then again, I too almost fell down the ditch when we finally reached it, but I managed to catch my balance and laughed my way to stabilization. That was until I noticed the new gift nailed into the smack center of the bridge. It was a paper in a frame. I tried to get closer until -

"Wait, wait, wait!" Jack hollered. "Close your eyes and latch together. I'll walk you over. This needs to be a surprise!"

"Jesus!" I hollered back as I did what he said. We all latched onto each other as he slowly walked us over.

"Alright, ready?"

"No shit!"

"Three, two, one, OPEN!"

We all yanked our eyes open in excitement to see a beautifully framed document from Princeton with a mini plaque on the bottom. It read, "Dear Veena Rosa, we are pleased to inform you -" but before I could continue reading, my mom screamed.

"AAAAHHH! OH MY GOD! SHE DID IT!" She clung onto Ralph as my dad grabbed me from behind and swung me around. We screamed in each other's ears, almost bursting our eardrums.

We got Jack involved in all the hugging and brought him into a big group squeeze. It wasn't until then that Mom started to cry. We all did.

"I can't believe it," I muttered. "I mean, I can, but you did it Veena." I tilted my head to the sky, not knowing where else to look. "You did it!"

"Jack, where did you get this?" Mom asked.

"I kind of kept an eye on your mail. Sorry. I know that's a low-key felony, but I didn't hear anything about you telling the schools of her passing. It came in November, and I thought that showing you today might be a nice surprise, and look!"

He pointed to the plaque at the bottom of the frame. It read, "Veena Rosa, Class of 2024. Pre-Vet Major, and Angel in our hearts."

Every gift was beautiful and so meaningful, but this one was my favorite. It was probably everyone's favorite now.

"I love it," my dad said with a tear in his eye. "But what did Sanders and Baron do?"

"Pay for the plaque and frame," said Jack without moving his focus from the framed document. Made sense, he ran out of money after buying his minivan. We all laughed as we continued to hug, cry, and smile. Veena's last and, what she would probably consider her biggest, success was out for everyone to see. My mom was probably gonna wanna bring it in the house at some point and protect it with all her might, but it was nice and meaningful to have it by the bridge for at least a little while.

"Hey," I said. "You know what other thing Veena considered herself successful at?"

"What?" Dad asked, almost immediately regretting asking.

"SNOWBALL FIGHTS!" It was true. That was the only part about the snow that Veena liked. I grabbed a ball of snow and smacked Jack in the face with it before he tackled me to the ground.

"Oh, YOU'RE ON!" Dad yelled, trying to find cover. He was always a strategic guy.

Within five minutes we were all drenched in snow, but I didn't notice. I was having too much fun and focusing too hard on my battle strategy. Then, a warm thought hit me like a snowball on fire. This was the first time we all laughed together since before Veena died. There was still such a long pathway on our grieving journey, but we were finally okay with not being okay right away. We were at peace with it.

I still contemplate to this day where I stand on faith. But doesn't matter. Wherever Veena is, she's *somewhere*. I never found out how this other world came to me, and I guess I never will, but it did. Maybe she has someone watching over her, maybe she's just keeping an eye on herself, but the last lesson that I learned was that it didn't matter where we are, I am going to see her again, and we are going to be laughing, just like she promised. And as we continued our ridiculous snowball fight, we all came to the same conclusion; Our family's laughter was the most infectious out of any family, and I knew for a fact Veena was somehow, somewhere laughing with us. I just knew.

Acknowledgements:

You did it! You finished the book! Look at you! Nova and I want to thank you first. Without my readers, it would be a pretty sad world, wouldn't it? You are the people that keep me going in everything that I do.

The next person I should thank is my dad, Doug. Without having a dad as an English teacher, I probably would have given up by now because I'm cheap. So, thanks for editing my book for free.

I also need to thank my grandmother, Adrienne for putting up with my god-awful stories that I wrote during our elementary homeschooling sessions on her type writer. I'm sure she still has every single one of them in her basement.

Thank you to my sister, Taryn who is probably reading this book for the first time five years after it's been published. Thank you to everyone who has ever read any of my writing and given me feedback. Thank you to Olivia for designing my amazing cover. Thank you to Ali for being the amazing friend that she is and posing for the amazing cover. Thank you to my mom and stepdad who were patient enough to wait and read this after it was published and after I screamed, "NO!" whenever they requested to take a peak.

And finally, thank you to Nova. My new best friend. Thank you for making me laugh and cry as we wrote this story together. I couldn't have done it without you even though you're not real and I made you up.

Made in the USA
Middletown, DE
04 November 2021